MW01139027

TIGER ISLAND

Reagan M. Sova

Harvard Square Press
Cambridge, Massachusetts

Harvard Square Press
Cambridge, MA
United States of America
ISBN: 9781521822159
Cover art by Jim Cherewick

Harvard Square Press
Cambridge, Massachusetts

harvardsquarepress.com

For C. H. & D. S.

& the love of my life, A. D.

TIGER ISLAND

COORDINATES

Preface

The Cooperative Commonwealth on the Tiger Islands was founded in 1872 by ex-communards from Paris, France. They were soon joined by former slaves from New Orleans, who established the archipelago's first school in 1882. With continued immigration from France and the U.S., the population of the independent, anarchosyndicalist commonwealth grew steadily throughout the 20th century, despite a U.S. embargo which lasted from 1901 until 1971. Perpetually self-governing, with a Francophone majority, the Tiger Island commonwealth has remained autonomous and democratic for the whole of its existence.

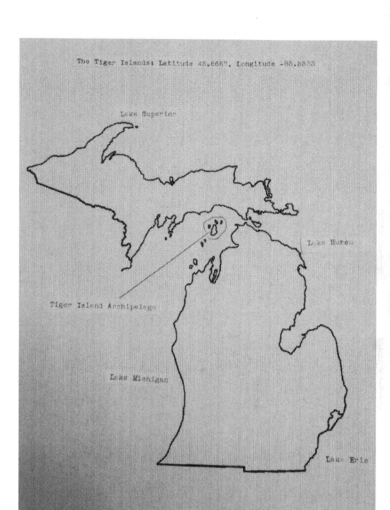

The Tiger Islands: Latitude 45.6667, Longitude -85.5333

Lake Superior

Lake Huron

Tiger Island Archipelago

Lake Michigan

Lake Erie

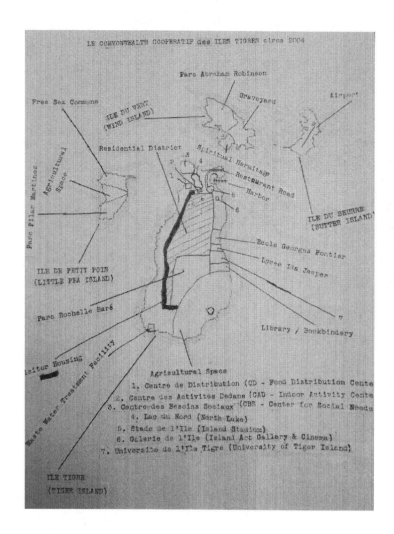

LE COMMONWEALTH COOPERATIF des ILES TIGRES circa 2004

Parc Abraham Robinson

Graveyard

Airport

Free Sex Commune

ILE DU VENT
(WIND ISLAND)

Agricultural
Space

Residential District

Spiritual Hermitage

Restaurant Road

Harbor

ILE DU BEURRE
(BUTTER ISLAND)

Parc Pilar Martinez

ILE DE PETIT POIS
(LITTLE PEA ISLAND)

Ecole Georges Fontier

Lycee Jin Jasper

Parc Rochelle Baré

Visitor Housing

Waste Water Treatment Facility

Library / Bookbindery

Agricultural Space

1. Centre de Distribution (CD - Food Distribution Center
2. Centre des Activites Dedans (CAD - Indoor Activity Center
3. Centre des Besoins Sociaux (CBS - Center for Social Needs
4. Lac du Nord (North Lake)
5. Stade de l'Ile (Island Stadium)
6. Galerie de l'Ile (Island Art Gallery & Cinema)
7. Universite de l'Ile Tigre (University of Tiger Island)

ILE TIGRE
(TIGER ISLAND)

5

Henri Sauvé
From an Undisclosed Location
Wednesday, November 2, 2011

CHAPTER ONE: It Takes a Stadium to Raise a Team

The pot finally boiled over a week before the stadium vote.

You just want your life story on the back of a cereal box, my father said, and the championship you keep yammering about - which, I don't even know what that means by the way. What championship?

He leaned against our egg-white kitchen countertop, arms folded across his chest.

Any major soccer championship. Maybe the Olympics because it's 23-year-old-and-under teams and not--

Are you kidding me? So I have to deal with your reclusive sister, who only speaks English now by the way, and then you come talking to me about stadiums *and* the Olympics?

May I continue? I said as diplomatically as a 15-year-old could.

He pursed his lips.

My team and I are trying to win a major championship, I said, to become linked together with this archipelago for all eternity. Is that too much to ask? It's not about my name in lights. It's a social goal.

My father adjusted the handmade wooden belt cinched around his green boiler suit. He'd never been violent with me, but the energy in the room suggested he might unfasten it and try to beat my ass.

You can achieve that through collective labor, he said; you need nothing more.

I frowned and nibbled at a buckwheat crepe. He proceeded to shout.

You know where Pinochet herded his victims in Chile, right before he tore them apart with machine guns? A stadium!

My nostrils flared, and my eyes rolled so hard one might have thought I was about to pass out. He continued, nearly at the top of his lungs.

The fascists packed in and sang nationalist songs and sent good working people to die! How can you be so appallingly unreflective? Yes, there's a budget crisis, but some stadium boondoggle is the last thing we need.

My father listed three things on his fingers.

Fascism, conformity, spectacle! Is that what you want our habitat to become?

He advanced towards me and stared me down, toe-to-toe, a foot away.

I won't turn a blind eye to it, he said.

Adrenaline coursed through me.

That's all I dream of, I said, fixed on the pupils in the center of those serious, circular Trotsky spectacles.

What's all you dream of?

You turning a blind eye to the things I do. You don't have to like me, or anything I do; just grant me a blind eye.

He gave me one last long look. My arms tensed, prepared, in case he lunged at me, but he strode out of the kitchen abruptly. Our creaky wooden stairs bore his heavy steps, and the door to his room upstairs shut quietly. I assumed he was preparing for his imminent work trip, touring wastewater treatment facilities in Cypress, because he stayed in there the rest of the evening until night. When I woke up the next morning, he was already gone.

***

500 people continuously occupied Parc Rochelle Baré for two and a half months until July 12, 1998, the day of the archipelago-wide stadium referendum vote. On that day, a beautiful sunny Sunday, 4,000 flooded the park with bread, cheese, wine, and banners written in French, slogans reminiscent of the student-worker uprisings in Paris some 30 years earlier:

Forget everything you've been taught. Start by dreaming.

Going through the motions kills the emotions.
Think about who has power over your life.

The one I saw most often said, *Commodify your party for free education and health care.*

Another variation, *Commodify your play for*

basic income and free time.

Despite the fanfare though, my teammates and I stayed subterranean in Gregor Heinrich's basement until four in the afternoon. A dozen of us huddled, shoved, sweated, and shushed around an 18-inch color TV. Our favorite team, *Les Bleus*, had a date with Brazil in the biggest football match on the planet: The World Cup Final.

A choir led the stadium in *La Marseillaise*. The French team sang arm-in-arm, *Aux armes, citoyens / formez vos bataillons...*

The room went quiet. Our teachers taught us to hate that song. Good working people, our anarchist forbearers in France, were hunted and killed because of the sentiments behind it. The song preached and glorified nationalist violence. At the same time, the French players were our heroes; Zidane, Henry, Trezeguet, and the gang - *Black, Blanc, Beur* - singing together in a country where Jean-Marie Le Pen and the racist, xenophobic right-wing always seem to loom.

Gregor turned to me and grabbed the bill of my cap. I remained unperturbed. He moved slowly towards me. Sweat beaded on his face. He whispered.

Our stadium. *Les Bleus*. How do you like riding this knife edge, sonny?

It's wild, I said.

We're living history, he said. Nothing's gonna be the same after today.

France kicked off against the favorite Brazil, whose iconic yellow jerseys were enough to intimidate opponents. The tension and heat in the Stade de France elevated as it did in our tiny, humid basement. My teammates and I all crowded the TV. Even soft-spoken Angel, our 17-year-old Zapatista captain who was still learning French, hollered, *Allez Les Bleus!*

Gregor shot me one more glance before he fixed his eyes back on the match.

C'mon, baby, he said, fist clinched. Today's our day.

***

Emmanuel Petit's shot in the final minute of play sealed the World Cup victory for France and propelled us to the surface, barreling out of the Heinrichs' screen door in a wild procession of shouting and cartwheels all the way to Parc Rochelle Baré. Once there, we settled into the massive late afternoon picnic. We scarfed bread and cheese and set up two-versus-two barefoot games with sandals and wadded t-shirts as the goals.

The sun disappeared into the lake, and the park cooled to sweatshirt weather. That's when the results of the stadium vote came in, at 10:22PM. Adèle Berman, lead spokesperson of the Stadium Movement, arrived at the park with an entourage and a bullhorn. She put herself together so well, and everyone seemed to recognize she could become our international spokesperson for the whole archipelago before she was 30.

Adèle stood up on a wooden chair steadied by two (literal) supporters. Tall lamps raised on ornate, green poles lit up the park, and one of them shone down on her. Etienne, our most senior player at 19, told the lot of us clustered only 20 feet away from her to shut it. She addressed the crowd through the bullhorn.

I have in my hand the results of the archipelago-wide referendum vote, drafted by the General Assembly, concerning construction of a multi-purpose stadium on Tiger Island, one half-kilometer southwest of the harbor.

We cheered with the crowd and quieted after a wave of shushes. I hopped on Gregor's shoulders piggy-back-style and shushed into his ear even though he wasn't saying a goddamn word. All 20 of us on the team locked arms or held hands. In the mass of my brothers, I thought, *Dear G-d, Hashem, Satan, whoever is in control, say the number. Just let her say the number we need.*

Such a silence fell over the thousands of students and workers gathered in the park that I swear I heard an owl.

Adèle brought the bullhorn up to her mouth again.

The results of the vote: 20,976 in favor.

She paused and looked up to smile at someone. I don't know who. Maybe her mother.

Cameras flashed all over the place.

And 20,215 opposed. The measure is approved!

5,000 voices erupted; hundreds of hats flew in the air. They rained down on me and my teammates in a celebration jam-pile for the ages. A 100-piece band with drums, tubas, trumpets, clarinets, hammer dulcimers, acoustic guitars, pots and pans, and everything struck up Auld Lang Syne and led several thousand people in an anthem that felt like New Year's, Hanukkah, Halloween, graduation, the finale of *It's a Wonderful Life*, and my birthday all at once. Young people kissed all over the place. I kissed an Asian girl I'd never met before and have never seen since. People uncorked bottles of Champagne, no doubt swiped from family cellars that afternoon. My teammates and I swigged straight out of the bottle and bellowed our team song for an hour among the throng.

All social games and popularity hierarchies seemed to disappear for the night. Lions laid down with lambs. Even a snobby art-rock girl a couple years older than me that my sister knew hugged me and said with exuberance, Henri, isn't this the best thing ever?

A drunk, ecstatic college kid from the Stadium Movement said to me at some point that night, Ok, now you guys just gotta become world-class, so all your matches will be sold out, and we can pay off that loan from the Danes in no time. Think you can do that?

Yeah, I said staring into space, a little buzzed myself. No problem.

Imaginary footage of us facing Brazil or France danced in my head.

Word floated around that night that our stadium would resemble Parken Stadium in Copenhagen, but smaller, with a capacity of 15,000. My vision was of a cold, blustery night, snow swirling outside; inside, a cozy, packed house was taking in a legendary David vs. Goliath match on real grass in a covered stadium.

The Champagne rapture cleared out of the park by three in the morning, except for a couple hundred people, who stuck around in small circles talking, smoking, and cuddling. Gregor and I set up shop in the grass under an old birch tree. We exchanged ideas, game plans, and dreams.

Ok, ok, this play is called Shark Heart. It's for a corner kick...

...and then we could play an afternoon match on Halloween in orange jerseys...

...No, no, she was like, I saw you. You totally just snake spit on that dude's neck...

At 5:15, the sun neared its return. Gregor's head rested on his hand. His eyes bobbed open then closed. A figure in the distance strode briskly past scattered litters of snoozing youth.

Ruth? I said.

It kept moving towards me.

Ruth, is that you?

My older sister stopped and stared down on me. My sleepy slits gazed upward.

It *is* you, I said, in a voice raspy from yelling.

She didn't respond.

We did it, I said, tiredly pumping my fist.

I half laughed and sounded stoned.

Oh my god, I said, we did it. *Les Bleus* won, and we're getting a stadium. We're gonna win a championship in it someday.

She stayed looking down at me with a stony-face worthy of a Buckingham guard. Her hair was all done. She wore makeup.

We're wanted at the Heinrichs, she said.

My demeanor sobered up. Gregor's parents were sort of in charge of me while my father was in Cypress.

They said it was very serious, she said.

I unfurled the blue sweatshirt I was using as a pillow. A sad looking beagle adorned the front of it.

Ok. Let me wake up Gregor.

Don't. They said just us.

My mind cycled through big bets and smuggled Playboys. All manner of mischief dating back a half decade flashed before my eyes.

Did they at least say what I did?

I asked that, but Mr. Heinrich said you haven't done anything. He told me it was urgent. They need to see us.

Henri Sauvé
From an Undisclosed Location
Thursday, November 3, 2011

<u>CHAPTER TWO</u>: <u>Everyone's Got Folks,</u>
<u>No Matter How Dead</u>

The day's first sunlight crept over the horizon while we passed row after row of the Swiss-style chalets that defined the architectural character of the residential district.

The parks union's gonna have a busy Monday, I said.

Ruth just kept her head forward and set the pace a step ahead of me. We'd traversed three kilometers at a steady clip when she tiptoed through the stone path in the Heinrichs' yard garden and knocked on their stained-wood door. I hung back, hoping they weren't home.

Entrez, we heard.

Dennis and Maude Heinrich gathered around the kitchen table with steaming mugs of tea. They did old school things, like get married. They were among the last generation on Tiger Island who did that in significant numbers. Usually, the mood at the Heinrichs was upbeat, but that morning, Dennis' eyelids hung low. He and Maude wore poker faces.

Ruth and I sat in the other two chairs. I didn't wait for opening remarks.

Ok, I said, we hardly had any champagne.

Gregor and I stayed up talking most the night. Nobody vomited. We--

Dennis put his hand up to stop me in my tracks.

Henri, Ruth, he said. Maude and I and our whole community care about the two of you very much.

Ruth blurted out, What happened to our father?

Dennis glanced at Maude with a gulp. She stayed quiet and the look on her face made me think of a sad puppy. He drew a deep breath.

Three hours ago, in the night, a minister in the Israeli government called the Diplomatic Counsel to report that a car in Jerusalem has blown up, in a bomb.

Dennis grew up in Rotterdam, and occasionally, he'd phrase things a little weirdly in French, his second language. I kept listening.

Your father, they say, was in the car.

A stillness blanketed the room.

Is he dead? I said.

Yes. I'm sorry.

Dennis paused, like he might say something else. I waited.

Life gives us these terrible mysteries sometimes, he said, and we may never know why.

My body got hot. The news made everything around me feel huge.

How do they know it was him? Ruth said.

The two Heinrichs locked eyes. Maude turned to my sister.

Dental records, darling.

Was anyone else hurt? I said, my voice wobbling.

Dennis shook his head.

No, Henri.

Tiger Island's newspaper of record - *La Gazette Populaire* (*La GP*) - would report the following day that the blast was so powerful it destroyed a shop full of birds. Twenty or so exotic birds died. Some died with the pressure waves and others perished from smoke inhalation while they flapped their wings in their cages.

In the kitchen with the Heinrichs and my sister, my face and body kept getting hotter.

Dennis grimaced after a silence and said, There's one more thing I should tell you. There's going to be some people from the Diplomatic Council taking your father's things. We've agreed to give them to the Israelis. They're investigating why this happened.

Do they think someone planted the bomb, Ruth said, or that he was trying to bomb someone else and messed up?

They just need to investigate, Dennis said.

An image of my father's things, ransacked, popped in my mind. I got up and stormed out of the front screen door without a word. They might have called after me, but I never heard them. I sprinted four kilometers flat out, from one side of the residential district to the other, back to my family's chalet.

Upstairs, in the doorway of my parents' former bedroom, I panted and stared for a while at my father's empty Cape Town Chestnut leather chair. He used to sit in that chair, reading, glasses perched low on the bridge of his nose. When I was a baby, with my sister and mother in her light blue nightgown, he'd read to us about historical figures like Guillaume de Beaulieu, Tiger Island's first inhabitant, who gave the famous November Speech of 1789, or Ida Jasper, a former slave from New Orleans who helped establish the archipelago's first school in 1882.

My breathing slowed with the reminiscence. I traversed the doorway and headed towards my father's credenza. The bottom two drawers overflowed with old letters from far-flung comrades. I found a photograph of my mother at a Passover Seder when she was young and happy. Some other ones were of her and her friends when she was in college in Dijon.

I scooped up the photos and plopped down in the leather reading chair. The sound of my breathing was all I could hear. My fingers ran across the nail-head studs of the chair, and for some reason I felt a tiny surge of anger. I got up to leave with my souvenirs, but when I passed through the doorway I stopped, thinking it might be the last time I'd see the room the way it was. My feelings softened. I doubled back and threw open his closet and smelled his clothes. Each camel hair sport coat and handmade maritime sweater, even the green boiler suits, I smelled them all. The pictures scattered on the ground while I was smelling and weeping so hard.

Ruth was waiting for me on the porch, her eyes red and bloodshot like mine. The sun was up. Older neighbors passed on their morning walks. The Diplomatic Council would be coming soon. I handed her the pictures. She thumbed through them robotically for a minute and gave them back to me. I tucked them under my beagle sweatshirt and parked myself next to her. With her gaze cast up ahead somewhere, she seemed to address no one in particular when she said, Both our parents are dead.

I shifted nervously on the chalet steps.

No buffer between us and the grave, I said.

Ruth rolled a cigarette and sparked it up with a lighter from London, Ontario. The smell of cig smoke reminded me of parties and calmed me a little.

Why was he even in Israel? I said.

I don't know, she said on the exhale. It's close to Cypress. He probably went for a weekend trip or something.

You don't think--

I got distracted. Our neighbor, Madame

Giroux, approached on an enormous penny-farthing bicycle. She held a nasty glare at Ruth while she drifted by on the big-wheeled, old-timey bike.

What the hell was that about? I said, sniffing.

Ruth stayed staring straight ahead and spoke dryly.

I think dad was talking shit about me to the Girouxes.

Really? Why?

She paused.

I'll tell you later.

I nodded, and my stomach grumbled.

Do you want breakfast? I can take us to Coeur de l'Aube.

With what money? Ruth said, her tone of voice becoming more grounded.

I won 40 bucks.

How?

Paul Feingold and this other kid, Maurice Jones, bet me 20 each on the World Cup. The fools took Brazil.

Ruth cocked her head, looking at me quizzically.

Give me those pictures of mom, she said. You'll lose 'em.

Bullshit I'll lose 'em.

Give 'em.

I bought us breakfast at Coeur de l'Aube by

the harbor and to this day Ruth can't eat lemon muffins without feeling sad.

***

My mother was a beautiful, raven-haired Jew who taught physically and cognitively disabled students at the *lycée*. One time when I was four, while she tucked me in, I said, *Maman*, what did your students do today?

They drew pictures of fish, she said.

Why did they draw fish?

Because they're learning about life in the lake.

The wobbling candlelight shone on her face while I searched her coffee chocolate brown eyes.

Do the other students at the *lycée* tease your students, *maman*?

She petted my black hair.

Not often, she said, misting up. You'll be kind to others when you get to *lycée*, won't you my boy?

Of course, *maman*.

I hugged her tightly.

Feel my muscles? I'm the fastest in my *crèche*.

When I turned five, I outgrew the *crèche* and started at the collaborative Deweyite primary school, and my mother brought me to the stony western beach of the island before my first day. She kneeled and spoke over a brisk wind.

Will you take care of this purple shirt, Henri?

She straightened my collar.

I made it special for your big day, she said.

Of course, *maman*.

Three hours after she dropped me off at school, a kid named He-Man knocked me off the climbing frame at recess. I fell six feet. The pain and shock of my shattered elbow caused me to blackout. When I woke up in the hospital, huge metal scissor blades chomped through the middle of my purple shirt. I strained my neck, surveying the damage.

My shirt, I said. You ruined it.

Shhh, the doctor said through a light blue surgical mask.

He put the scissors to the side on a tray full of silver instruments.

We'll buy you a new one, he said quickly, his words muffled.

My mother and father rushed to the hospital during my surgery. Ruth too. Supposedly, all the doctors and interns who viewed the x-ray said, *Clear amputation, move on to the next*, but one surgeon, Dr. Kenyon, who I met years later at a cocktail party, lobbied for pins and plates instead. He saved my arm.

Ruth brought me a stuffed animal of a cat in a tuxedo, and my father helped me pee into a bed pan. From a chair at my bedside, my mother read me *Charlotte's Web* in French and petted my head all night.

The following evening, the four of us ate mutter paneer, my favorite meal, and perused get-well cards from all my classmates. Even He-Man wrote me one. No one yelled at anyone the entire time.

***

A man walking his dog found my mother's body on the western beach on May 4, 1989. The coroner discovered an aneurysm and ruled out foul play. My father laid in bed with me in the dark, trying to quiet my wailing.

Go to sleep Henri, he said, his voice cracking.

When my team started playing bigger matches, internationals, I never got hung up on the question of whether or not she'd've been proud of me. I like to think she'd at least have had enough compassion to grant me a blind eye. Something else haunted me about my mother's death though, some other question. I'd burst awake sometimes, cold sweating and trembling from a nightmare about it. When I was in Jamaica in March of 2000, right after my 17th birthday, I asked someone.

A 30-something woman, Tanish, chatted with me at a dance hall in Spanish Town, and before long, our conversation bounced from soccer, to the music of Sister Nancy, to the supernatural.

Have you ever talked to the dead? Tanish said.

No, I said, but I'd like to. I'd like to talk with my mother.

A serious look came to her face.

I talk to the dead all the time, she said. I have a gift for it.

For real?

Yes, for real. And I have my own website. You don't believe me?

Well, I said, I couldn't-- I mean, I do believe you have a website.

She gave a *tsk* and reached into her pocket.

Her card said: *Tanish Henry. Medium.*

I looked back up at her and said, My name's Henri too, but with an *I*. My first name, I mean.

She slugged her drink and set the glass upside down on the bar.

Alright, Henri with an I, she said. You can call or email me. And since you're a soon-to-be-famous footballer, I'm taking 10% off when you set up a session with me. But I should be charging double because everyone who comes says it's an experience worth its weight in gold.

I told Gregor about my run-in with Tanish later that night in the lobby of our hotel.

You should totally do it, he said, examining her card.

I smirked, a little floored at his suggestion.

But it's fake.

Of course it's fake, he said, but it could be awesome. Coach Thomas said we're here also to meet people and to listen to them.

Gregor turned towards Etienne's younger brother David, surfing the web for $15 an hour on the hotel's computer.

Davey, he said, Henri and I need to look up this website and send an email real quick.

***

After our 2 - 1 win against Jamaica's U-23 squad at Independence Park the next day, Gregor and I knocked on the door to Tanish's house on Cypress Drive in Spanish Town. Coach Thomas reluctantly gave her blessing on the condition that we bring a burner cell phone and return to the hotel before 11:00PM. Gregor held a jar of jam in one hand and jackfruit in the other. I had a bottle of Appleton Estate rum tucked under my arm, along with the cash for Tanish in my sock. I expected a house filled with strange clocks and jars and baby doll heads with candles on top of them, but when Tanish answered the door in a simple orange dress, all I found stepping inside were baby blue walls and modest décor, family pictures and stuff. She was a custodian at the University of the West Indies, in addition to her home business as a medium.

She cooked us barbeque chicken and seemed pleased we ate so much. We drank goat's milk and a little rum and talked about her home village called Snowdon. Then she set up 20 candles of various sizes and colors, lit them with a single long match, and served me a thimble-sized mug of steaming ayahuasca tea. She said, *Drink it*, and turned off all the lights.

Twenty minutes passed while we sipped tea in the dark, listening to a Sam Cooke record.

I could only see Tanish's silhouette, but I heard, *Are you ready?*

Yes, I said, with heavy eyelids and a solemn countenance.

What's her name?

Esther, I said.

Tanish's voice boomed low.

I'm reaching out to you Esther, mother of Henri. He's here, a young man who has words for you.

She shook her fists on both sides of her head with her eyes closed. Her bracelets jingled, and the candles all danced and cast a glow on her purposive face. Gregor and I exchanged an intense glance. His perspiration mustache glistened. Tanish uttered soft, indiscernible words for a half-minute before her big white eyes sprung open, staring into mine.

I have her here, she said, motioning to her right. Speak, child.

I hesitated. Nervous sweat beaded on my forehead. Gregor noticed me struggling, bogged in a million thoughts. A minute is a damn long time to sit tongue-tied during a séance.

I might lose her, Tanish said. She's next to me, but she wants to stay only a little longer.

My first day of school rushed to my mind, the day my mother straightened my shirt with a backdrop of waves and morning sunlight. The smell and sounds of the giant lake crept into my senses, then a bitter image on the shore: cool freshwater sloshed against her lifeless body and jet-black hair.

Tanish and Gregor seemed to beg me with their eyes, as tears stood in mine, like rabbits ready to bolt. Gregor put his hand on my shoulder and squeezed.

It's ok, brother, he said.

The image broke, and my eyes rose to meet Tanish's.

I want to ask her, I said slowly, At the end, was there any pain?

The room became very quiet. Tanish sank back in her chair. She looked to her right and nodded as if listening to someone. To this day, neither Gregor nor I can explain how she could have possibly known this, but after a moment, Tanish turned to me and said, Esther tells me no pain. She says she went to the beach and woke up from a dream.

***

With the news from Jerusalem about my

father, the guardianship question fell in my lap. Ruth had won a fellowship for study in the MFA fiction program at The New School in Manhattan, and we talked about me going with her one night, but in the end, we both knew my destiny lay on the island, with the team and the new stadium afoot. And New York intimidated me. I pictured myself stabbed or shot, dying in the street, busy executives shuffling around my corpse.

I helped her bring her luggage to the harbor, and we hugged goodbye.

I hope you can come visit, she said. I don't know if I'll be back very often.

How come?

Not everyone's had as much fun here as you have, she said, with a bittersweet smile.

I wasn't offended by this. My life was quite fun, all the time.

And I get the vibe dad poisoned the well a little bit, she said. You know how the island's like one big kibbutz.

I nodded but inside still puzzled a little. After our mother died, my blessed boyhood ignorance and rowdiness guided me forward, in a new family: my soccer team. Ruth faced the world in a different way, with books, music, and depression, and my father always seemed resentful that the collective wasn't good enough to heal her wounds. He didn't understand the distinct ache and void at the core of a motherless girl. I didn't much myself, but at least I didn't judge.

But maybe if you come back, I said to her, we can make some fun times, like a new chapter.

I'll write to you, Ruth said, hugging me once more before she navigated the slender ramp from the dock to the ferry.

She appeared on the upper deck of the vessel while it coasted through the waters of the lake.

Bon voyage, I said, waiving feebly, wanting to yell, *It's nobody's island but ours!*

***

All the other adults in my family, except my grandmother in Montreal, were dead, and my aunts and uncles who I barely knew lived far away on the west coast of France, so the Heinrichs became my guardians for my final three years as a minor. In the past, Gregor and I had proclaimed, usually arm-in-arm with wicked teenage grins, *Yep, we're brothers*. But in August of 1998, when I moved in and signed the papers, actual legal credibility now bolstered our fraternal assertions.

We fell into a productive rhythm and never fought. He lived upstairs in his own room at the top of the chalet, and I lived downstairs. Dennis acted like it was no biggie to surrender his basement office. I slept like a stone in that cold dark cave.

In the '98 - '99 academic year, Gregor and I spent full days at *lycée*, followed by five-hour practices with the team. When we got home around 8:30, we'd wolf down the elder Heinrichs' victuals and do what we called Study Table until 10:45. Gregor delved into Geography and graphic design that year, and my specialization in *MacGyver* and *Dukes of Hazard* Studies deepened exponentially.

On a brisk Saturday one week before Halloween, Gregor and I yard-camped in a tent behind the chalet. We talked about the future, and in the process, ventured into some deeper territory.

I'm gonna tell you something I've never told anyone, Gregor said. You know how my parents adopted you?

Yeah.

They adopted me too, he said. I've been adopted my whole life.

I thought about what that meant and pondered its significance.

Do you know who your birth-parents are?

No, but I'm gonna find them. I need to know why they didn't want me.

I smirked and said, No one wouldn't want Gregor Heinrich.

But they didn't! And they never came back for me.

I swallowed a big gulp of air, nodding. I'd known Gregor since I was seven and he was eight. He'd seemed bulletproof the whole time. Until that night, I'd never known what it was like to feel sorry for him.

We both zipped our sleeping bags and put our heads on our pillows. Some minutes of silence passed. I didn't know if he was still awake.

I stayed for you, I said, and no matter where I go, I'll always come back.

His sleeping bag unzipped, and he protruded his whole arm. He held it out to me, with no words. I knew what to do. We hooked our right-hand fingers and pulled them in opposite directions, hard, while pressing our thumbs together.

Championship, I said.

Championship.

The friction made a loud snap.

Henri Sauvé
From an Undisclosed Location
Friday, November 4, 2011

CHAPTER THREE: A Dude Awakening

Back when we played American high school teams, a truck driver at a highway rest stop in Vulcan, Michigan once asked me how we did.

We got the win, sir.

Oh yeah? Who'd you play?

Norway High School.

Oh, ok. How big did you guys win?

10 zip, sir.

He paused, listening to the clip-clop of cleats on pavement.

Which one of you got the touchdown?

Oh, we play soccer.

Oh, he chuckled. Wrong football.

Later that summer, after we trounced eight other high schools by similar tallies, the sports-writer for *The Traverse City Record-Eagle* attributed our success to what he called our *once-in-a-generation, freak-level speed*. Coach Thomas poured gasoline on the fire when she instilled in us second-nature, one-touch passing. By the fall, there wasn't a high school team in Michigan that could keep us under five goals. Before half-time.

Local papers and AM sports talk shows around the U.S. and Canada buzzed about our shut-out season. From July to October of '98, in sixteen matches, we never surrendered a single goal. After we topped the Michigan Wolverines men's varsity team 2 - 0 in Ann Arbor, I stood up on my seat in our rented short bus and waived a t-shirt over my head like a helicopter. My team-mates filed in one by one, drumming on the seats and whooping.

Who's next? I said, high-fiving Gregor and Etienne, ruffling Lucas' mop-top and slapping David on the ass, hard.

He whipped around, grimacing.

Ouch, motherfucker!

By the spring of '99, our squad of 16 to 20-year-olds had graduated to university exhibition matches exclusively: one weekend we'd be in Madison, Wisconsin driving home headers against the Badgers, and the next we'd be in Min-neapolis working the give-and-go to fell the Golden Gophers. I asked a Michigan State mid-fielder if the East Lansing crowd on hand was usu-al for them. He cocked his head.

Are you kidding? This is the most people we'll play in front of all year.

The packed stands brought college recruit-ers and minor sponsorship offers. Coach Thomas opened a team bank account for our cut of the ticket sales, and after transportation costs, we voted to spend our surplus on team kits from the island sewing cooperative. They designed our uniforms: plain white t-shirts with red numbers on the back, plain black shorts, and white socks with four thick, red, bumblebee-style stripes going up them.

With a new, official look, our squad emerged still unscathed after ten friendly matches against major university teams.

I'd like to get a sense of what you're feeling about our next moves, Coach Thomas said to all 15 of us, gathered in the covered bottom deck of a ferry returning to the island. Do you have a desire to keep training and playing at this level? How far do you wanna take this?

We'd defeated top-ranked Ohio State 3 - 1 in Columbus the previous day.

I'd like to go as far as we possibly can, Gregor said from a table for two, looking around to gauge our responses. Whatever the next level up is, I think we're ready for it.

Second that, I said. Enough with friendlies, I think we should find a league or a tournament and win a championship.

Yesss, David and Lucas said, exchanging glances, each of them leaning against one of the large starboard windows.

Everyone nodded or gave some indication of approval.

Ok, Coach Thomas said, so I'll come clean. We've discussed it before, more in the abstract, but I've been seriously researching the possibility of an Olympic bid for us.

Eyes bulged and faces beamed all around;

the room had turned electric.

But something to keep in mind, she said, we'd be the first team ever to represent the islands in anything. Some people might not like that.

My head reared back so far I got a double-chin.

Why not?

Coach Thomas shrugged and took a seat.

Because that's nationalism. That's big business. As it stands now, it takes a lot of violence to organize the Olympics.

I rolled my eyes.

There's also the question of your parents, she said. Most of you are still minors.

They'll come around, Gregor said, with a hint of defiance.

After a pause, Etienne piped up from the back, the only one of us standing. He looked straight at Coach Thomas.

Is this what you want?

Coach Thomas pressed her hands together and took a deep breath.

I'm not sure if I've ever told you all this, she said, but when I got hurt at the end of my first year [playing professionally] in France, and no team signed me after I recovered, I was devastated. Sure, I got to go back home to Martinique, but that wasn't how I wanted it. Everyone I'd known since youth had high hopes for me, and when I came back, well, I was a bust. Imagine everyone you've ever known putting a hand on your shoulder with a sad face, like, *Sorry you failed.* I couldn't even watch soccer on TV for three years.

Over the constant hum of the ferry's motor, we listened intently, our eyes fixed on her.

When I stumbled onto a bunch of rag-tag boys playing in the park, I never dreamed two years later, we'd be at this level. You've given me a second chance with the beautiful game.

Gregor squinted, nodding with a face so solemn it almost made me laugh.

When you chase a dream, Coach Thomas said, I've learned it's a risk.

She leaned back in her chair and glanced out at the lake for a moment before she turned back to us.

But if you're all in, I say let's do this.

We destroyed our throats celebrating and got shushed by the ferry's porter.

***

Four days later, Coach Thomas called an evening meeting in the General Assembly chambers. In one of our team track suits from a stately, lacquered wooden podium, she addressed all us players, along with 28 irritated-looking parents and guardians in the room. She presented our case, spinning the benefits of an Olympic bid.

After the meeting adjourned, we could tell many of the parents still seemed skeptical, so we composed and delivered personal letters to each one, begging them to consent. They eventually relented, but the one caveat they insisted upon was that Coach Thomas write a report and present it at century's end, detailing and demonstrating the ways soccer enhanced our political knowledge and engagement. She agreed. And it planted an idea in her mind. Near the end of May, she told us.

With the purses from our Big Ten friendlies, she said, we've built up a tidy team *bourse* (account).

We packed into her concrete-walled office inside the gymnasium of *Lycée Ida Jasper* where she taught physical education. Black team warm-up jackets like the one she was wearing littered her desk, along with stacks of Olympic qualification paperwork and a half-dozen of our official uniforms.

So if we're serious about Olympic qualification, she said, here's what I propose: an eleven-week trip, from August to the end of October, to South America.

Hell yeah! I yelled.

I doled out high-fives and shoved people. Joseph, our striker, beamed ear-to-ear, his gold front tooth glinting. David tumbled out of the office with Georges, our goalkeeper, while both punched the air in celebration.

When our jubilation subsided, Gregor put his hand up before anyone.

Motion for consensus, he said.

Consensus, I shouted, following suit with my hand above my head, before all 15 of us raised our hands to indicate collective agreement.

Coach Thomas grinned. She'd already put in hours of leg-work.

Ok, she said, good. The plan coming together is that we'd play a series of matches against semi-pro and smaller pro teams, but I'm going to present this to the school and to your guardians as a study abroad experience because you'll have to miss the first quarter of the fall semester. That means most our time off the pitch will be spent learning from people engaged in political struggle.

That sounds awesome, Etienne said. I'm writing a research paper on the International Monetary Fund in South America for my Global Studies class.

Angel chimed in enthusiastically.

Oh really? I got a Noam Chomsky book I could lend you about how the IMF imposes all these...

My eyes glazed over. The thing that irritated me most as a youngster on Tiger Island was that people connected politics to goddamn everything. Teachers had this refrain that made me wanna barf: *And how does that help the collective?* Often, I'd turn to see if I could catch David or Gregor's eye, so I could mouth the words: *Fuck the collective.* Where I came from, that was like a Catholic school kid saying *Fuck Jesus.* Soccer became my escape and hideout, and I didn't want it infiltrated with talk about politics.

I snapped out of a daydream about my biggest crush, Chantal Goya in the film *Masculine Feminine* circa 1966, when I heard Coach Thomas say, You're already skilled, 26 wins and 0 losses shows that, but I promise, you'll improve on the pitch exponentially. The game they play in South America, you haven't experienced it yet.

Now there's some breadcrumbs I can follow, I thought.

***

Coach Thomas summoned her colleagues and our parents and guardians to another presentation in a small science auditorium at the school. She invited all of us too. By this time, presentations like these must have seemed like old hat to her. The parents and teachers discussed the trip afterwards, without her and us, and we were all to meet at Coach Thomas' office the next day at noon to get the word.

The big news about the South America trip is this, Coach Thomas said.

We waited, hypnotized. She held up a receipt for 16 plane tickets.

I've got dibs on an aisle seat, she said.

We hollered inside and around the door of her office.

Dennis Heinrich told Gregor and me that Coach Thomas had presented such detailed research on the global justice movement in South America, groups with whom we could meet, that she'd convinced enough people in the room. Along with school-sanctioning, a grant from the *lycée* padded our team funds.

The summer brought warmer weather and even more excitement. The archipelago IWW and the Danish crews ramped up construction so they could complete the stadium by the fall. Coach Thomas spoke before the General Assembly of the whole archipelago and requested sanctioning of our Olympic bid. We were surprised and stoked when they issued a prompt yes. Despite my 14-hour academic/athletic grind each day, and my ideal sleeping conditions in the basement, everything coming together with the team and the stadium kept me wired all night. At the same time though, throughout that academic year, an empty feeling lurked inside me when I thought about Ruth.

We never had a fight, but we hadn't talked in a year. Even Hanukkah came and went. Some of Ruth's Hanukkah parties have now passed into legend. The year she and her friends pooled together two grand to have Ira Kaplan (of Yo La Tengo) fly in and play a set flanked by two huge flaming menorahs, classmates and kids older than me who'd only ever teased or ignored me, begged me just to hear the details. Ruth invited me to her other parties too at the island art gallery, and she always told me to invite a couple friends. She'd introduce Gregor, Lucas, and me to the cool older kids in the art-rock bands, no shame in her eyes on account of her little jock brother & company.

In early August, I picked up the Heinrichs' black rotary phone, and my first conscious memory bubbled up amidst waves of dial tone. Ruth and I, ten and three respectively, pounded the keys of an expensive grand piano at my maternal grandparents' chalet. I wore blue overalls, no shirt underneath, and an oversized straw hat. Seated next to her on the piano bench, I thought, *I like this person. She's helping me make more noise.*

The Heinrichs' receiver beeped off the hook, and I put it down.

Maybe I'd be in a better position to mend the distance between us, I supposed, after I returned from being as far away from home as I'd ever been in my whole life.

***

Even though I couldn't speak Spanish with the workers in the *empresas recuperadas* (recovered factories) we toured around Buenos Aires, I could see the upswing of morale on their faces. The capitalist bosses had shuttered their factories, citing insolvency, but the workers took the places over and started producing essential materials like nuts, bolts, and containers. Sitting cross-legged with my teammates on a dusty cement factory floor, I listened, for once, to every word from the speakers.

I was kind of blown away when one of the workers at an *empresa recuperada* called Los Galapagos said they drew inspiration from the IWW 5/5 system practiced on our island: five hours of work each day, five days each week; five months on, five weeks off. I wouldn't've guessed people all the way in Argentina knew our archipelago even existed, let alone the collective prerogatives of our workers.

During the Q & A of our last factory visit, I asked one of them, a mustachioed young man in a boiler suit, how footballers could help community-run syndicates.

Footballers, Coach Thomas said, translating for the man in real time, professional ones at least, are in a unique position because they have vast social power, and because people already feel like they have an ownership stake in the club they support. They say, *we won* when their city's club wins, even though they didn't play the match and some capitalist bosses reap the profits. So my advice for footballers would be to draw from that ownership mentality so many already have and use community-run syndicalism to structure the team itself.

I nodded, receptive in spirit, if a little foggy in understanding.

And, he continued still through Coach Thomas, footballers can always donate to syndicates and groups fighting to transfer power from corporate tyranny to local communities. So don't forget about us when you all get big-money contracts.

We chuckled along with the speaker.

Be football Robin Hoods, he said in accented English.

***

We started on the outskirts of Buenos Aires, playing four matches in three weeks and training at least five hours every day. We ate dinner with workers and activists in the evenings and had slumber parties in their living rooms before we moved on to Santiago, Chile, repeating the process there. Round three commenced after we boarded an aging Embraer plane, which we all teased Coach Thomas about.

Look at this old jalopy, I said. You're taking us on a suicide mission.

So she's got a little character, Coach Thomas said.

She stretched her arms with a victorious smile when we touched down in the massive alpha metropolis of Sao Paulo.

We kept to playing second division professional clubs, no slouches them, but still we finished 11 - 0 after ten weeks on the continent. Our final test of the trip would take place in Bolivia against one of the best clubs in the whole country, the first division leaders Club Jorge Wilstermann.

Two days before the match, we got to stay

in a hotel, and Angel laid on one of the twin beds, reading a Bolivian newspaper. Georges, Gregor, Joseph, and I formed a semi-circle around the television, making fun of a Peruvian talk-show called *Laura.*

Holy shit, Angel said.

My neck craned away from the television. What?

This article is about our match. It says there's been 20,000 tickets sold already.

We greeted the news with a small chorus of *Ouahs.*

Angel read on a bit more and said, Check this part: *Club Jorge Wilstermann will face an exciting, youthful squad from Tiger Island who are unbeaten but also untested. Sunday's friendly match promises to be the hottest ticket in Cochabamba this weekend.*

He glanced up from the paper, impressed with what he'd just read.

You hear that? David said, standing in the doorway, wearing nothing but jeans with big ol' holes in the knees. All y'all better cool it with the sex and candy.

He proceeded to serenade us with the Marcy Playground song, for no apparent reason.

On the eve of the big match, we practiced light on a pitch in a public park and visited a nature reserve, feral, full of vegetation, run by a non-profit who tended to sick or injured animals. Gregor and I fed an Andean Bear whose arm was in a sling, and later, a young lady strolled past us, smiling, walking a leashed puma who appeared to have one of its eyes gouged out.

In the evening, we piled back in the bus after our dinner of *tucumanas* and mac & cheese and went to meet with 16 local water activists at an elementary school a couple miles from our hotel.

They were part of a larger community group, called Cochabamba Socialists, who did all sorts of solidarity projects from feeding the city's homeless children to supporting community ownership of various city services. Their actions injected the demands of working and poor people into the city's political conversations. Most of them worked as teachers and factory laborers, and some were high school and college students. That night, they explained why the water situation was their most pressing concern.

The speaker I remember most within those orange clay walls, and can still see in my mind's eye, was an 82-year-old former sugarcane farmer named Marta. Pain and fire radiated from her weary, sun-leathered face. A foot taller than her, Angel stood next to the woman and wore a solemn countenance. She spoke Spanish softly. He interpreted: My country, Bolivia, has privatized railways, telephone, air travel, and now water.

She spoke more, softly still.

We owe the World Bank and must transform our country, the papers say, but I agreed to no loan. And I distrust the privatized models. Now I must pay 60% more than a year ago for water from a handcart.

In a classroom filled with 15 frequently ridiculous boys, freakishly good on the pitch, on the eve of their biggest match to date, one would've heard no sound but Marta's little voice. She shouted abruptly and cried.

I am old and poor, Angel said, interpreting her words into French. Too old to farm. I cannot afford 60% more when I could barely afford the original rate. I get such headaches from dehydration. And my clothes, even now, are dirty. I cannot spare water to wash them. Every creature should have water. Thank you.

Gracias Senora, we said in a scattered chorus.

My wide eyes followed her in silence as she tottered back over to the right side of the room. She leaned against the wall next to a young Bolivian boy.

Out in the parking lot afterward, Etienne suggested a plan he seemed to have snatched from the air that evening. We never debated *If*, only *How*.

Let's tell Coach Thomas, Etienne said, after we get back to the hotel.

When the bus dropped us off, he asked her if we could have an impromptu team meeting.

Ok, Coach Thomas said, a little curious.

We piled in and around the two couches in

the hearth of the lobby.

So you said our trip was financed through the team *bourse* surplus, Etienne said, and the grant from the *lycée*, and then our three paying matches here.

That's right, she said.

And that we're already on the plus side for this trip.

Yes.

Well, we'd like to donate our purse from tomorrow's match to Cochabamba Socialists. We'll build up team funds from our matches in the stadium once we get back home.

Coach Thomas, who'd shushed us after lights-out the night before, found us looking quite serious, clad in a patchwork of thrift-store t-shirts and shorts.

And, David said before clearing his throat, we were wondering if you could give it to them after we've left the continent. Maybe we could wire it to them or something.

Coach Thomas brushed a stray dreadlock from her eyes, which seemed to be misting.

Damn you boys, she said.

We laughed and broke into small applause.

Yeah, I said grinning, let's get that grandma some water.

***

At our sold-out, South American finale, with the majestic Bolivian mountains in the distance, 25,000 spectators in the Estadio Felix Capriles bore witness as we emerged from the tunnel. Tall blue and red flags, the Wilstermann team colors, swayed back and forth in a sea of dancing and singing. A plume of red smoke rose from an especially spirited section of the stands. People danced in it and pounded drums. Up to that point, we'd never seen a crowd like that, and it was our first contest against a club as good and as physical as Wilstermann. But we swung the ball fast and played as a unit.

A mid-fielder on the outer right-wing, I hung back in our third for most the match, helping Paul and David in defense. Even with the extra support in the back, the Wilstermann forwards still ripped three shots on goal. One hit the post and two forced Georges to make miraculous diving saves, the best I'd ever seen out of him. The score could've easily been 3 - 0 in their favor at half-time.

Gregor and Joseph, our strikers, were stymied up front for the first 80 minutes. A stalemate seemed to be coming on. Near the 81st minute though, Gregor trapped a bouncing loose ball I'd poked away from one of their strikers, and I sprinted the other way, towards their goal. With two players closing in, Gregor managed to hit Jules, our science-genius mid-fielder, in stride. Jules swung it over Etienne on the left-wing near half-field, and Etienne lobbed an aerial pass to me going forward, up the center, on an overlapping run.

I burnt one defender with a flick of the ball to the right and then cut it back left to get around another. In a one-on-one with the keeper at a bad angle near the touchline, Joseph, who'd streaked from half-field to the 18 in three, maybe four seconds, entered my periphery. I chipped the ball up high enough, a foot higher than the keeper could reach, and Joseph snapped a header with pace, on target, to put us up 1 - 0.

The score held ten minutes later when, before a stunned, quiet crowd, the ref blew for final time. Coach Thomas bulged her eyes and whisper-shouted at us, No jam pile! Be gentlemen!

Filing back in the tunnel though, she became like the rest of us, whooping and busting random dance moves.

We flew the whole next day from Cochabamba to Bogotá to Toronto to our airport on Butter Island. Up above the clouds, with the match-winning assist in my back pocket, one might've thought I'd've still been hyped, laughing non-stop, bouncing around the cabin and getting shushed by flight attendants and passengers alike. Instead, I just peered out the window for a bit. Decompression and reflection time. I wrote in a journal about Marta and the people we met. In the window seat to my right, Gregor designed the first prototype of our team crest on the back of a barf bag.

The finished version was a red and black shield that resembles the city crest of Paris, for our founding native-Parisian inhabitants, but repurposed in its colors and three symbols across its top banner. A *fleur-de-lys* sits on the left, for the Black Americans, former slaves from New Orleans who built a new life with the ex-communards on Tiger Island. A Star of David is on the right, for the influx of Jewish émigrés (including my mother's parents) who came in the 1930s and 1940s and doubled the population of the archipelago at the time, to 30k. And in the middle of the crest's top banner, you'll see an Anarchist circle A, which represents the values and practices that we strive for.

In the aisle seat to my left, David leaned over and whispered.

Can you believe millions of gallons of saltwater are just sloshing around a couple kilometers below us?

I nodded sleepily.

I wonder if all of us are thinking about water, I said. I was just thinking about Cochabamba Socialists. The whole trip, really.

Yeah, David said. I feel like I've just taken a sip from a fire hose.

***

My big team duffle bag hit the floor of my basement room when I noticed a wrapped, addressed box on my dresser.

Dang, fan mail already? I thought.

But then I read the return address:

Ruth Sauvé

636 W. 16th Street Apt. D

New York, NY 10011

Etats-Unis.

Gregor hollered from upstairs, Yo dude, you want something to eat?

Yeah, thanks! I'll be up in five.

Inside the box was a brown paper lunch bag filled with half a dozen overdubbed tapes and a letter, a key for navigating the them.

Maybe ten, I said, shouting upstairs.

I lifted the phone off the receiver.

Ruth Sauvé
636 W. 16th Street
Apt. D
New York, NY 10011
Etats-Unis

Henri Sauvé
C/O Gregor Heinrich
27 rue Camille Pissarro
25600 Tigre Ile

30 August 1999

Dear Henri,

Just wanted to drop you a line to say that I'm going to be a mother, and probably will not be cool for much longer. So I'm passing the torch of some of my favorite music of my 20s to you, as you'll be there soon enough.

The Skinny

*Royal Trux – certainly their worst album, which begs the question, "Why am I even sending this?"

*Tool – again their worst album. Actually it's not bad. It's just overshadowed by the greatness of their second album AEnima.

*Dubbed mix tape – some of it's crap, some of it's decent. The sound is bad because it was all record-ed from 7" records. My faves: Royal Trux – Shockwave rider, Zeke – Chiva Knieval, White Trash Superman – Couldn't (if I tried)

*Mercury Rev – you know...

*Sonic Youth Dub Tape – Sonic Youth's experi-mental jet-set, trash, & no star. After that it's all manner of crazy (mostly Siouxsie and the Ban-shees, I think) because it was made by a mentally tortured houseboat dweller who gave me the tape, as well as LaVey's "The Satanic Witch," for Valen-tine's Day. So, I won't be held responsible.

*Sonic Youth – Confusion Is Sex. This came out the year you were born!

*Pavement – Slanted & Enchanted. Low-fi royal-ty. It gets a little warbled around Conduit for Sale, but after hearing the rest of the album, you might think, Does it even matter?

*Chemical Brothers – Bass heavy techno trip-hop. Features Beth Orton of Portishead & Noel Gallagher of Oasis. Best track – Setting Sun (fea-turing the aforementioned Noel G.) Maybe take it to a party or something?

*EPMD – Business Never Personal. One I withheld from your boyhood salad days. Still the most underrated rap duo you're liable to come across.

*Spacemen 3 – An album for & about tripping acid, although I am NOT advocating drug use. It listens just fine as a sober, relaxing ambience. If you don't like it or feel the urge to give it away, sell it, lose it, use it as a Frisbee, DON'T. I will gladly take it back. The last time I checked it was pretty dang hard to find.

*Sonic Boom – Spectrum. Sonic Boom is from Spacemen 3. I have owned the CD for about 8 years & quite inexplicably have never listened to the whole thing.

*Pixies – Doolittle. Ever wonder where Nirvana got it? If you like this one I can loan you my VHS of them playing at Brixton Academy in 1991.

I heard about your trip and thought you might enjoy some traveling tunes (or not). Maybe you could feed the tapes to a hungry Culpeo in Argentina?

Love,

Ruth

Henri Sauvé
From an Undisclosed Location
Saturday, November 5, 2011

<u>CHAPTER FOUR: Crest, Tumble, and Run</u>
Joseph, Gregor, Jules, Lucas, David, Etienne, and I wrapped on the door of Ruth's Spanish Harlem one-bedroom. A maiden voyage to New York City for each of us. We'd bought maps of the city, compasses, and bottles of pepper spray - a more practical choice than my proposed idea that we should all carry swords. Ruth opened the door and party sounds spilled out in the hall.
Her jaw dropped.
You're here!
All of us boys cheered and raised our arms triumphantly.
Hanukkah Sameach, we said, hugging her one-by-one and gleefully piling in.
We were greeted by eight of her New York friends who studied creative writing at the New School, and I noticed Ruth had a pot of potatoes and onions and a bowl of flour all set up for me. With no hesitation, I drifted to the kitchen and commenced preparing latkes like in years past. The first four sizzled in a pan of oil when I peeked in the living room to see Etienne and Joseph locked in an excited conversation about Isaac Asimov with a couple of Ruth's friends. Sounds of music, laughter, and voices washed against me.

Have one off the first batch, I said, motioning Ruth to the kitchen. The host has to have 'em piping hot.

She came over and stuck a fork into one before swirling it in a dollop of apple sauce.

Mm, she said after tasting. You haven't lost your touch.

I glanced at her big belly, six months along. She had the air of someone redeemed.

So tell me about this little feller, or gal, I said, gesturing to her stomach.

He's a feller, they tell me, Ruth said.

She grabbed a couple ultrasound pictures from the fridge and held them up to me, so I didn't get my greasy mitts on them.

His silhouette was lined with currents of blue and light green. I thought of aurora borealis and wondered who he'd be.

What's his name?

Arthur.

Arthur, I said, nodding approvingly to her. That's a championship name.

She put the picture back up, and I scanned the room.

Who's, um, who's the father?

Ruth smiled with a slight grimace.

There's been an agreement. I'm keeping it private. The only person I'll tell is Arthur, when he's 18, and he can do with the information what he wants.

I became lost in thought for a second.

That's what you want?

Definitely.

And him?

Oh yeah, she said with an eye roll.

She didn't seem to have a flicker of doubt. I wiped my hand on a rag and put it on her shoulder.

You'll do great, I said. I'm proud of you.

We hugged.

And I gotta say, I said, about everything, I'm sorry if--

Ruth waived her hand and addressed me by my childhood nickname I hadn't heard in a decade.

It's ok, Hen. It's been a weird year.

I nodded.

I'm glad you came tonight, she said. The boys too.

I peered around the corner at everyone again.

It's a new generation on the island, I said. Did you know we're gonna try out for the Olympics?

Yeah, Ruth said, tossing a couple latkes in the pan. I've been reading about it on the internet. Congratulations.

Thanks. Coach Thomas even quit her job at the *lycée*.

Ruth's eyebrows jumped.

Wow. She must really think you guys can do something.

I think so, I said. I could see us going far.

Ruth flipped the latkes with a spatula.

I'll finish these up, she said. Enjoy the party.

I joined the others, and before long, Lucas and I had devised a whole new dreidel game: how many chips can you stuff in your maw while the dreidel's still spinning? The miracle of the night was that neither of us vomited during the living room dance party. I had such a blast I didn't stop yammering about Hanukkah until Tu B'Shevat.

The day after we qualified for the Olympic Games in Australia, defeating the U.S. 1 - 0 on their home turf, the call about baby Arthur came. We still had one more match, the final versus Mexico, but I flew from Pennsylvania back to Tiger Island, where Ruth decided to have him. She gave birth to him alone, with just doctors and nurses. I was the only one who came to greet the boy. The whole team was back in Pennsylvania, and her few island friends had scattered around the world.

Mom would love him, I said, holding the little bundle.

Ruth's skin looked like paper, but she mustered a dim smile from her hospital bed.

Uncle Henri, she said.

Arthur stirred. His tiny fingers blew my mind.

I hopped on another plane three hours later and headed from Butter Island to Toronto to Harrisburg, PA before catching a taxi back to Hershey. A sea of green Mexico jerseys swayed in the crowd that day. Hoping to play spoiler, we went up 1 – 0 with 61 minutes gone by. Magic swirled in the air around me, thirty minutes from an undefeated qualification campaign. But they struck a free kick-from 30 yards out, and it ping-ponged around in the box before finding its way into the back of our net, tying the match.

Four minutes later, one of their midfielders threaded the needle to a streaking striker with blond hair down to his butt. He took a touch and torched Georges from 22 yards out. The pass should've never gotten through though. A step away, I just couldn't propel myself there in time. I should've asked to be taken out at 70 minutes when my left calf started to cramp.

After the goal, David collapsed to his knees while three ecstatic Mexicans ran past him high-fiving and celebrating. He grabbed two huge fistfuls of grass and yanked them from the earth while his eyes bulged like a psychopath. He screamed bitterly and unintelligibly.

Fuck me, I thought. *That's one of my best friends since four-years old, and I caused that.*

I nearly cried I was so frustrated and ashamed, but I stayed in the match. I was determined to get the ball back and score if I had to take it off one of my own damn teammates. But I

63

couldn't. And time ran out. Mexico dealt us our first loss ever, 2 - 1. In the locker room and on the bus, Coach Thomas and my teammates spared me any supplemental kicks to the balls. They knew I knew.

Paul found me in the last rear seat of our chartered team bus, slouching. I hid underneath sunglasses, a Florida Gators visor, and enormous cans over my ears. He tapped on my shoulder.

Hey, Henri.

I startled and pulled my big headphones down around my neck.

Do you blame yourself for the match?

Yes, I said.

Don't. We're gonna get 'em next time. We're going to the Olympics. Bigger fish to fry, you know?

I nodded, appreciative.

Thanks man.

Paul stood up but before leaving, he said, My shitty tackle led to the free-kick that tied the match. How do you feel about me?

I shrugged and looked up at him.

I love you.

There you go, he said. That's how everyone feels about you.

***

Because of the anti-child, anti-family social and economic conditions in the U.S., Ruth decided to stay on the island to raise Arthur. With the two of them back, and all of us on the team barreling towards our goal of becoming champions, something deep within me felt whole again. Where the ideological friction remained, however, was around the stadium. A group comprised of 60s radicals and younger primitivists who'd voted against it continued to grumble. They weren't interested in seeing Rage Against the Machine christen the place on Halloween, nor were they keen to attend the Y2K NYE dance party with Chumbawamba. But while the anti-stadium contingent considered these events annoying, our Olympic bid was an affront to their values.

In our inaugural home match after qualifying, we faced Bolivia's U-23 team, and dozens of hopping mad protestors bought tickets. They streaked buck naked across the field at regular intervals, interrupting play six times. Field control smothered them with blankets and carted them away while they screamed, Get your hands off my body, fascist! Fuck patriarchy! Fuck the Olympics!

I thought for sure the Bolivians would make fun of us, and after the fifth time, I jogged up to their captain, the goal keeper.

Sorry about all this *amigo*.

No worry, he said. It's nothing.

He squirted a green water bottle into his mouth. The Bolivians were cool. Goodwill remained from our visit there ten months before.

Over the course of 90 minutes, we put together three times as many scoring chances as they did, but the match ended in a 1 - 1 draw. I love the post-game photo of me mugging with a huge grin, my arm around David; Gregor can be seen scowling in the background. Something about seeing him so young and so pissed off cracks me up to this day. The poor feller wanted to win so badly in our first big homecoming match.

A week later, when the sun came up the day of our big rematch with the U.S., protestors chilled outside the stadium, having vegan cook-outs and forming drum circles. They seemed reasonable, and their food smelled good. I'd just become vegetarian and was tempted to ask if I could join them. By kick-off at 1:00PM though, they ran wild, many of them naked, inside and outside the stadium. Worst of all, they lobbed sour milk balloons at our bench, our fans, U.S. fans, and anyone else in the way.

Play was interrupted over a dozen times. Field control probably got a better workout than we did that day. Numerous fist fights broke out around the stadium between our protestors and U.S. fans, and our protestors and our supporters. A kid in a black bloc took a swing at a U.S. fan in a Bush-Cheney t-shirt, and the American smashed a bottle of Rolling Rock over the kid's head. He had to go to the hospital for stitches. Our Peace Monitors, unarmed volunteers with walky-talkies to summon other Peace Monitors (or defense forces if someone had a gun), recorded a dozen other instances of violence and intervened in countless more scuffles.

Consistent with the bedlam around the stadium, the match itself poked our team's morale in the eye. The U.S., licking their wounds from the qualifying tournament, jumped out of the gate as aggressive as one might've expected. At ten minutes, the U.S. captain Chad McCarty swept David's legs out from under him while they vied for a 50/50 ball. The British referee cautioned the American with a yellow. Two minutes later - I should have seen this coming - Gregor, not only our leading scorer but the closest thing we had to a team enforcer, body checked McCarty to the ground during a contested header. He really hammered him. McCarty's writhing seemed genuine. The ref reached in his pocket while I jogged over.

Now, now hold up, I said futilely. He was going for--

My stomach dropped when he pulled out a red card. Gregor would be suspended for our Olympic opener. And in the match at hand, we were down to ten players. The Americans' first goal came a minute later, and they added another before half-time. The second half brought two more goals, neither of them ours. In front of our first sold out crowd in the Stade de l'Ile, we suffered our worst loss to date, 4 - 0.

A sour milk balloon exploded a foot in front me and soaked my shorts with a minute to play. Their star mid-fielder, Landon Donavon, jogged past me with a smirk. He struck me as the type of guy who spends time in a tanning bed. He whipped around.

Hey, he said, is every game on Commie Island this big of a shit show?

I thought about it in earnest.

No.

I added, Well, this is only our second match.

He tipped his head back and cackled, trotting down the pitch. But he wouldn't be laughing his way to Sydney. That's what Coach Thomas reminded us after the match.

We learned lessons today, *right?*

15 dour faces gathered around her in our dressing room. We nodded slightly, a few of us seated in folding chairs.

Lessons about letting adversity get to us, she continued. Lessons about losing our tempers and treating everyone with respect. We learned these for when we're on bigger stages, right?

Ouais, several of us said.

Gregor gave a sheepish nod.

She went on to discuss some things we could've done better with ten players. On her way out the door, she said we should go to bed early because we'd be meeting at the harbor at 7AM for a 15-kilometer run and that we'd be sprinting like crazy for the next two days before our flight. With big cans over my ears, I retreated into a tape of *Julius Caesar* by Smog and thumbed through a zine about endangered tigers I'd bought from one of the zine vending machines outside the stadium.

A boulder-sized weight rolled off my shoulders when I exited the Stade de l'Île at twilight and found all the U.S. fans had left. Our spirits stayed up as much as they could for the next couple days. Based on the tsunami of criticism in the papers and from friends, parents, girlfriends, boyfriends, and basically everyone except precious baby Arthur; it seemed a trip to the other side of the planet was probably the best thing for our battered team at that juncture.

Our precious young minds never could have fathomed.

CHAPTER FIVE: Eels in Sydney

Up to our big Olympic opener, my team-mates and I had never encountered the likes of Andrea Pirlo. His speed and strength reminded me of that terrifyingly fast and deadly extraterrestrial critter from *Predator*, the Schwarzenegger movie. Maybe Gregor could've hung with him, but Gregor was still zipped in his track suit on the bench, serving his one-match suspension. Pirlo netted a hat-trick in the first half, then they just seemed to trickle in from the rest of his Italian teammates. 14,000 spectators, along with folks all over the world watching on TV, witnessed goal after punishing goal. The Italian coach reclined on their bench, smug as a preacher who knows he's going to heaven.

The ref, in an act of benevolence, concluded the match at 90 minutes on the dot, with no stoppage time. For the final tally, the scoreboard read: *Italy 10, Tiger Island 0*. The day had turned so surreal I half-expected Salvador Dali-esque elephants with long, spiny legs to pour from the dressing room tunnel. During post-match interviews, maybe a journalist's microphone would melt.

Not even Coach Thomas had much to say

71

afterwards. Gregor kept his head down. No one was in the mood to clown. I checked the stats after, and we never even made a single shot on target. Our opening match collapse was so severe that when Conan O'Brien made a joke about it during his monologue, his audience didn't even laugh. They all just went, *Awwwww*.

Criticism flooded in from every direction imaginable. Back on the island, voices condemning our contribution to the orgy of corporatism, nationalism, and militarism seemed to gain steam from our embarrassment. The mainstream sports media yucked it up over the 10 - 0 score line. Talk of men among boys, etc.

As the Aussies say, we carked it.

***

From his bed in the hotel, in a fluffy, white monogrammed bathrobe, David eyeballed Jules, Lucas, Joseph, and me playing cards and said, Who wants to drink some of this lousy, cut-rate gin with me?

The next day, Coach Thomas ran us so hard David puked, though so did Paul, just from the intensity of it. Gregor scowled throughout the whole six-hour ordeal and retreated to our room immediately after the mini-bus dropped us back at the hotel. I poked my head in the door.

You wanna go swimming with us?

He pumped a 20-pound dumbbell, his face fire-engine red.

Nope, he said without even looking up at me.

Outside of our angry, grueling practices, Coach Thomas whispered on the payphone in the lobby. For three-hour stretches in the days leading up to our second match, she'd be murmuring, scanning the room, with scratched off long-distance phone cards strewn all over the little shelf. Joseph had a theory she was plotting an escape and would leave us to coach ourselves. The rest of our team moped, sore physically and mentally. No one would even play me in ping-pong. I had to play tourists.

In a rematch of the qualification finals, we squared off against Mexico and played like sweaty, beleaguered salesmen. The stench of desperation swirled around all of us. I got a yellow card in the first ten minutes for tripping one of their strikers with a greedy tackle. Gregor blasted impossible shots on goal from forty-some yards out.

We finally got a glimpse of a chance at 79 minutes when Lucas threaded Joseph a beautiful ball from midfield. Joseph, with only the keeper to beat, launched a rocket of a shot from just inside the 18, and it rose high but knuckled down and drilled the top crossbar. The ball shook the goal-frame and sprung up, back, over and out of play for a goal kick. The TV replay showed Joseph's reaction in slow motion. The announcer said, *You can see the exasperation on his face. They've come so far and are just so desperate for a goal.*

Gregor and Angel each hit the post too. *Three times* we hit the post in the final ten minutes. With stoppage time 60 seconds away, Freddie Rios, Mexico's hard-nosed golden boy, got lose. His teammates strung together a few crisp passes, and he snuck a shot in the lower right corner of our goal. 32,000 people erupted after 89 minutes of mostly calm. Our boom-ball panic intensified in the embers of the match. The Senegalese ref with whom I'd spoken French during warm-ups filled his lungs with air, put his whistle in his mouth, and forced the air back out.

I collapsed to my knees and toppled over in the grass. We'd put our chips all in and got summarily cleaned out. Eliminated.

***

With one match remaining in the group stage, and nothing to lose, our team morale hovered back above sea level. We mugged for tourists snapping pictures at our practice and even signed autographs for a few youngsters in the hotel lobby. Gregor and I restored our glorious ping-pong rivalry during our last night in Sydney while Paul, Georges, Lucas, and Etienne hung out in the adjacent lounge, talking and trading zines. David strolled in, clean-shaven with wet hair, wearing his bathrobe again, as well as the hotel slippers.

Hey everyone, he said, Coach Thomas said to meet her in the Bob Hawke conference room.

74

We all perked up.

Now? Gregor said.

Yeah, David said slicking back his light-blonde, shoulder-length hair. She called my room and said to gather everyone there for a meeting with a special guest.

I excitedly looked at each of my teammates.

For *real*?

I ain't messing, David said.

We milled around the conference room for nearly an hour, speculating as to whom might walk through the double doors, but Coach Thomas slipped through them alone, looking somewhat forlorn. We watched her approach, disposable cameras in hand.

Everyone, Coach Thomas said with a shrug, sorry to cause a stir and keep you all waiting, but our guest had to cancel last minute.

Is that why you've been on the phone so much? Joseph said.

Coach Thomas nodded.

I thought this person could help get our morale back up after the loss, she said.

Who is it? Gregor said intensely, like he was about to track them down and kick their ass.

I snuck a glance with Jules, and we stifled laughter.

Ya know, Coach Thomas said with heavy eyelids, it's not important.

I agree, Etienne said loudly.

We all turned to him.

Fuck 'em, he said. This is who I came to take pictures with.

He shoved his camera a foot from my face and pressed the button. I flinched at the flash, and everybody laughed. I charged the flash of my own Fujifilm throwaway and said, Ooh, now you fucked up.

Etienne hid behind a chair. Flashes started going off all over the place. We developed the film before we left Sydney. There was the picture of Etienne peeking out from behind a chair; one of Gregor, Coach Thomas, and me arm-in-arm; and Etienne ordered four of the now-classic shot of me, startled, pulling a stupid face while David and Joseph cheese in the background. I pulled out all those pictures and looked through 'em once every hour on the plane ride home.

***

In our final match, the Czech Republic claimed a 1 - 0 lead on a quality header, but we'd created a couple more chances than they did. Coach Thomas brought us in close during half-time.

Listen to me, she said. What you do in these next 45 minutes is gonna determine how you remember these Olympics for the rest of your lives. I think we'll be back, playing on a stage like this again. But you know what? Nothing's guaranteed. Everything you have. Leave it out there. 45 minutes.

At that point, during half-time of our third match in the 2000 Olympics, we'd failed to score in our previous three and a half matches. Nothing in the first half here, nothing against Mexico the match before, nothing against Italy, and nothing against the U.S. back home. That's 315 minutes of live play; five hours and 15 minutes of striving and sweating and yearning, with nothing but a big ol' bagel on the scoreboard under Tiger Island.

Not two minutes out of the half-time gate, I lined Gregor a pass from mid-field. With his back to their goal, he greeted the ball with a nifty touch and created some space for himself on the right side of the pitch. He turned and blasted it from 20 yards out. The shot bent left. The keeper dove but it curved left some more. The ball rocketed off the left crossbar and bounced right, into the back of the net.

The American ref cautioned us for excessive celebration.

About ten minutes later Angel had a ball fall right in his bread basket off of Etienne's pin-point perfect corner kick. He drove his laces through the ball, low, low, low, and hard, scoring off the full-volley.

Near the end of the match, Gregor got tripped from behind in the box. Half the Czech side mobbed the official, pleading their case, but he pointed to the spot and didn't budge. Gregor rose to his feet, picked up the ball, and tucked it under his arm. He swaggered my way.

Gregor has the best hair, I thought as he approached.

He shoved the ball in my gut and leaned in a centimeter from my ear.

All you, motherfucker.

With the ball on the spot, I surveyed the crowd at the Melbourne Cricket Ground, the mass gathered to enjoy some sunshine and have a nice time. I galloped to the ball after the ref's whistle and struck it to my left. The keeper dove, guessing correctly. He might've even gotten an outstretched finger on it, but the shot had pace. It glided past him by a millimeter. High-fiving my brothers and hamming for the crowd, there I was at 17 years and 211 days: the youngest player to score a goal in modern Olympic soccer.

***

In the locker room after our lone victory, we chanted *Rotto! Rotto!* We were slated to spend our last three days in Australia on Rottnest Island a.k.a. Rotto. We rode bicycles around the sandy, low-lying island and viewed shipwrecks in a glass bottom boat. A bikini-clad, strawberry blonde-haired girl my age read *The Great Gatsby* on the beach the morning of our last full day on Rottnest. I inched up to her beach towel and recalled the only part of a class discussion on Fitzgerald's masterpiece that I hadn't slept through.

Pardon me miss, I said, but do you think Jay Gatsby is a Christ-figure?

She laughed. We chatted for a bit and playfully quibbled about who would defeat whom in ping-pong. She said her name was Tiarne.

I'm Henri, I said. I'm with those fools.

I gestured to my teammates, splashing and wrestling in the ocean.

We just finished our first Olympic campaign in soccer, I said.

Tiarne invited me back to her parents' houseboat for lunch with her, her older brother Max, and her parents, all from Perth originally. We carried on in the open sun about quokkas, Tiger Island, Perth, and Rottnest. Max asked me if I saw Eric Moussambani from Equatorial Guinea, the swimmer who swam so slow compared to the others but who won hearts with his determination.

I heard about him, I said.

The mother jumped in the conversation, In the papers, they called him Eric the Eel. That's his nickname now.

The father added a thought, with no hesitation.

I didn't watch the match, he said, but from the highlights, versus Italy, you all played like a *whole team* of Eric the Eels.

He laughed, and Tiarne rushed to my defense.

Dad, your nerve.

The mother put her hand on my forearm.

I'd take it as a compliment because your team and Eric the Eel-- I admire people who persevere.

Tiarne gave me a knowing smile. I got the overwhelming feeling I was gonna lose my virginity later that night. The father set down his apple daiquiri, seeming flustered.

Well, that's of course how I meant it, if I could've had a chance to finish.

In that moment, I decided I liked the whole family. We hobnobbed for an hour until I had to leave for a team meeting at three. Tiarne walked me from the dock back to the beach, and we held hands. I hugged her before I left and both our hands joined.

Can I see you tonight at nine? I said.

She frowned.

We're leaving at five.

Leaving?

For Perth.

I tipped my head back, grimacing.

Damn floating houseboat, I said.

She leaned in with her cheek on mine and whispered, Will you write to me?

Our heads pulled back slowly, cheeks never parting, and our lips met under the sun.

I smooched an Olympian, she said with a

playful grin.

I kissed the tanned freckles on her cheek beneath her soft eyelashes, and then her lips once more. She produced an address book from her backpack. I wrote to her when I got back to the archipelago. We pen-paled every couple of months for a year but our letters tapered off.

***

Splashed across the third page of *La GP*, the headline said, *Sour Homecoming*. The picture shows Jules, Ezra, and me all pulling stupid faces, ducking the sour milk balloons that rained down on us as we stepped off the plane. Georges and Angel quit the team the next day. I grilled them at the team meeting.

What's the deal?

Angel shrugged.

We went to the Olympics and got crushed, he said. We reached our limit.

Georges concurred.

We had our fun, but it's time for other things.

Ezra expressed doubts he was ready to fill Georges' shoes. David informed us he was taking three months off. Coach Thomas proposed an indefinite hiatus which I wasn't sure would ever end. As some sort of consolation for our team falling apart, Etienne invited Gregor and me over to his chalet and got us blown-out-high for the first time in our lives. Gregor played FIFA '98 on

PlayStation in the basement.

I feel like I'm controlling the players with my mind, he said, laughing uncontrollably.

I slaked my cottonmouth upstairs in the glow of an open refrigerator. Blue Gatorade dripped from my chin onto my heaving, bare chest. David stepped inside the kitchen screen door with a bottle of wine and a paper sack of shucked corn. He flipped on the lights and rumpled his nose.

Where's your shirt? And what's up with your hair?

What about it?

You look like you've just been electrocuted, or struck by lightning.

I touched my greasy black mop, which was standing straight up. It felt perfectly fine to me.

Why'd you quit, Davey?

David scoffed and set his wine on the kitchen table.

I didn't, he said.

I closed the fridge and took another long pull of the bright blue liquid.

We were supposed to do something, I said, and now it's all crumbling.

David twisted a corkscrew into the bottle.

Well, he said, we still might get another shot in four years.

He looked me up and down, a derisive smirk on his lips.

That is if you don't crack up first.

He meant go crazy. I busted up laughing for a spell that continued even after David had traded his smile for a troubled look of concern.

The Olympic Men's Football Team of the Cooperative Commonwealth on the Tiger Islands

Games of the XXVII Olympiad
2000 – Sydney, Australia

Roster

No	Name	Position	Age
#1	Georges Disi	GK	19
#2	Gregor Heinrich	F	18
#3	Maurice Jones	D	18
#4	Joseph Atem	F	18
#5	Paul Feingold	D	17
#7	David Lefebvre	D	19
#10	Angel Rojas (C)	F/MF	20
#12	Jules Solomon	MF	18
#13	Etienne Lefebvre	MF	21
#24	Nicholas Cohen	D	19
#55	Henri Sauvé	MF	17
-Reserves-			
#00	Ezra Taga	GK	16
#0	Lucas Dujardin	MF	19
#3	Jupiter Agoot	D	18
#25	Benjamin Berman	D	16

Coach: Abeba Thomas-Dupont

Group Table
Group B

	Pld	W	L	T	GF	GA	GD	Pts
Italy	3	3	0	0	16	1	+16	9
Mexico	3	1	1	1	3	6	-3	4
Tiger Island	3	1	2	0	3	12	-9	3
Czech Rep.	3	0	2	1	2	9	-7	1

Group Stage
14 September 2000
Hindmarsh Stadium, Adelaide
Attendance: 14,060
Referee: Diego Torres (Argentina)
18:30   Italy   10 – 0   Tiger Islands
        Pirlo 5'
        Pirlo 12'
        Comandini 17'
        Pirlo 29'
        Ferrari 32'
        Ambrosini 35'
        Gattuso (pen.) 41'
        Ambrosini 62'
        Ferrari 71'
        Comandini 78'

Group Stage
17 September 2000
Brisbane Cricket Ground, Brisbane
Attendance: 32,760

Referee: Jonathan Faye (Senegal)
20:00 <u>Tiger Islands</u>   0 – 1   <u>Mexico</u>
                                   Rios 89'

Group Stage
20 September 2000
Melbourne Cricket Ground, Melbourne
Attendance: 22,670
Referee: Maxwell Peters (United States)
13:00 <u>Tiger Islands</u>   3 – 1   <u>Czech Republic</u>
                                   Heinz 42'

      Heinrich 47'
      Rojas 59'
      Sauvé 83' (pen.)

Henri Sauvé
From an Undisclosed Location
Monday, November 7, 2011

CHAPTER SIX: When the Past Struck Back
    During my one and only class at the University of Tiger Island, I listened to a heated discussion about the CIA-backed coup in Chile, which took place 28 years before to the day, on September 11, 1973. The conversation jogged memories of my father castigating me for my support of the Stadium Movement. An image of the Chileans we'd met on our South American trip flashed into my mind too. Their hands were up. Bullets sprayed into them. The Japanese professor from next door made an abrupt, bombastic entrance and snapped me from my daydream.
    There's been a major attack in New York! Airplane crashes! We're all watching history unfold in the assembly room!
    I splintered off from the group and hightailed it back to Ruth's little chalet on the southern end of the Residential District. At her writing desk, she caught sight of me through the screen, rapping my fist outside.
    Ok, she said annoyed, opening the door. Enough with the cop-knocking.
    You gotta turn on the TV, I said, rushing past her.
    The South Tower had just collapsed when

we turned on her rabbit-eared set in the kitchen.

Oh my God, she said. I gotta call Berta and Hugo (her best friends in New York).

She frantically dialed numbers on an old-fashioned copper wire. My heart pounded. Ruth held the phone to her ear before hanging it up seconds later.

The lines are jammed, she said.

Arthur cried from the back bedroom. She went to get him. My cheap ol' flip phone rang. It was Gregor.

Instead of *Allô*, I answered, Are you seeing this?

Gregor yawned.

Seeing what?

My eyes bulged.

Turn on your TV!

Which channel?

Every channel!

He flipped on the TV, and we watched together for a speechless minute, holding the line. Someone leapt from a hundred stories and tumbled end over end all the way down.

Gregor and I gasped.

Holy shit, he said quietly.

My neck, head, and jaw felt like they were on fire, fizzing, filled with Coca-Cola. The feeling came on quickly.

Hey, I said, I-- I gotta go.

My phone's little battery pack went flying

when it hit the lacquered wooden floor. I joined it there a moment later, sliding down with my back against one of the lower cupboards. Ruth returned with Arthur in tow to find me holding my head like some of my brain was trying to escape.

Are you alright? She said.

Little Arthur puzzled at me without a sound. Even he could tell something was up.

Get him out of here, I said with an angry wave of my arm. I don't want him seeing me like this.

Their eyes widened. I crumpled in a ball on the floor, said a tearful goodbye, and instructed Ruth to call an ambulance.

***

In November of 2001, Gregor signed a two-year contract to play for the Chicago Fire the following spring. At 19, he was the first member of our team to turn pro, the first person in the history of the archipelago, in fact. He moved to the Windy City in January of '02 and found me a month-to-month rental in Logan Square for May and June when the season started. I was in the stands for him every match, clapping, destroying my throat, except during the two and a half weeks I spent in England and France.

Stoke City F.C. and Paris Saint-Germain each invited me to try out with them in the second half of May. Something was off though from the minute I landed over there. A sharp pain shot through the center of my head the night before my first day with Stoke. An occasional burning sensation churned in my lower left abdomen after dinner. The Coca-Cola fizz returned to my neck and jaw while I was on the train to Paris. Two of the episodes ended in embarrassing, false-alarm trips to the E.R.

In the French capital, before my two-day tryout with an ailing PSG, I ransacked my notebook of contacts, breathing rapidly. The phone rang five times and went to Gregor's voicemail. Ruth, David, Joseph, Etienne, Lucas: none of them answered. I leaned my back against the filthy, smudged glass of the phone booth, staring at Coach Thomas' name and number.

My island teammates and I still played pickup games and lifted weights together, but we hadn't had an official, full-team practice in one year. I wasn't even sure if our team still existed (or persisted) or if Coach Thomas remained my coach. And even then, she wasn't my buddy, therapist, or mommy. I was ashamed to have her hear me in such a state, but I didn't want to leave the earth without saying goodbye to someone I knew and cared about. With each ring, I secretly hoped I'd get kicked to voicemail. She answered on the fourth.

Allô?

I full-on lost it when I heard her voice. The familiarity of it left me aching for a boyhood that seemed to have vanished around the same time as those towers.

Coach, it's Henri. There's been-- I think--

I was hyperventilating.

I think I've had a brain aneurism. My right arm and the right side of my head-- There's shooting pains, and weakness.

Hey, hey, listen to me.

She spoke with intensity but compassion.

Can you see? How's your vision?

I can see, I said.

Have you fallen? Can you walk? Where are you?

I can walk. In a phone booth.

You walked there?

Yes.

I wiped away tears and snot with the back of my hand.

Oh, Henri. I think you're ok. It sounds like you're having a panic attack. Breathe deep, in and out. Close your eyes.

My stomach puffed up big, and I held it. And down it went on the exhale.

Maybe I am, I said. I keep having 'em.

Through my stuffed nose, a laugh of relief escaped me.

You must think I'm insane.

No, she said. Believe me when I say, I've made this very call before. I'm 34, and I made this call to my mother two years ago, in fact. I've been half a world away from all my friends and my parents for most my adult life now. I know how hard it can be.

She listened to me breathe.

But I know it must be-- You miss your parents, don't you?

I nodded, my face fully scrunched. I held the phone away so she wouldn't hear. The picture in my head was of my mother and father on their honeymoon, in front of the Hemingway house on Key West. They're both as tan as they'd ever been in their whole entire lives. My father's sideburns explode from the sides of his head and corkscrew over his giant glasses, all the way down to his lower jaw. My mother beams with both arms around him, her hair radiant, shiny-black. They were both still in their late 20s. I think what destroys me about that photo is the unbridled joy on their faces; they're happy and smiling with no idea of what's about to hit them.

On the other end, Coach Thomas said, I want you to do something.

Ok.

I need you to take three deep breaths, I'm gonna do 'em with you, and then I want you to run one kilometer, as fast as you can, and call me back. People who've had brain aneurisms, or strokes, or heart attacks can't run a kilometer in three minutes. They just can't. Only you can prove to yourself you're ok, but I want you to use your body to show your mind that you're ok.

I sniffed.

What if I collapse and die?

If you can't jog even, then ok, tell someone to call an ambulance. But I'd bet my life you're not gonna collapse and die today.

I survived the episode and showcased my best, most intense play during the tryout. A vision of returning to my coach and friends with good news and a healthy head fueled my performance.

After a red-eye flight back to Chicago, the Blue Line bobbed and rumbled my jet-lagged, famished body all the way to the Logan Square Chicago Diner. My hand pushed the door open to some vegetarian Country Fried Steak when my phone rang its head off, an unknown French number. I couldn't answer. The call went to voicemail while I stood outside the diner, attempting to calm the butterflies. I listened to the message. It was them.

In my mind, I chanted, *P-S-G, P-S-G, Ho-lee fuck*.

I returned the call.

Is Coach Lugo available?

I got transferred, and he picked up.

Henri, are you ready for good news?

A native of Portugal, his French wasn't half bad.

I love good news, I said.

Good. Here it is: we'd love you to join us in

Paris this year.

Tears of joy rained on my Chicago Diner fake steak while I wolfed it, smiling and laughing to myself up at the bar. The bartender could tell I was a total mess, and he leaned on the counter in front of me and lowered his voice.

You alright man?

Yeah, I said. This stuff is just so good. What is it? Seitan?

Yeah, it's just battered and fried seitan.

I love it, I said, dabbing my eye with a napkin. I'm just, so thrilled to be alive.

***

PSG and I struck a three-year contract on the 26th of June in 2002, and I moved to Paris on the first of July. They gave me the league minimum, 108,000 Euros per year, and I was ecstatic. I didn't have an agent and didn't want one. To me, the deal was, you get a boatload of Euros to play a game you love in a city you wanna explore. My only question was, where do I sign?

On my first full day back in France, at my studio apartment near the Jaures metro stop, two kilometers from the Parc des Princes where we played, travel fatigue plunged me into a coma around two in the afternoon. Thirteen hours later, I woke up newborn-lamb groggy, fumbling for my Walkman. It hummed on my chest while sounds of *The Natural Bridge* by Silver Jews leaked from my over-ear headphones. I stared at the stucco ceiling, hesitating to explore my new city in the dead of night. At first light though, my ass was out the door, wandering all over the place.

By 9:25, nine kilometers of pavement had flowed beneath my feet, and I'd purchased a *croissant*, two *pains au chocolat*, an Orangina, a green apple, a raspberry yogurt, blue cheese (by accident), and a solid spruce-top Washburn acoustic guitar. Parisians passed, hurried and beautiful, while I watched them through the window of a Montmartre brasserie at lunch. That's when it hit me just how far I'd be from the archipelago for months and months: Ruth, Arthur toddling around and giggling with a head full of curls, and all my friends. I'd just had a good two-week stretch in Chicago, with Gregor and my big news about PSG, but all alone, questions and doubts pounded at the gates.

I wondered to myself from my café table for one: *What if I suck and get released? Am I out of shape? What if I get in a taxi, and it explodes? Or what if my heart, for some inexplicable reason, stops beating and I die on the pitch in front of fifty-thousand people? Or what if I have a brain aneurism and die on the street alone, with no one watching? Whoa, my heart's beating fast now.*

My hand rose to feel my chest.

Oh shit, I said to myself. *Am I having a heart attack right now?*

The pounding confirmed it.

Holy shit. I am. This is it.

An Australian fella in his late 30s eyeballed my guitar case.

You speak English?

I nodded quickly, sweating.

What's in your case? Are you a player?

I clutched a fistful of my sweatshirt and chest.

I think I'm having a heart attack!

My face, I'm sure, was angry and red. The man fetched me a paper lunch sack from behind the bar.

Breath into this, he said.

I heaved deep breaths in and out while the sack puffed up and down. He patted my back and squeezed my shoulder like Gregor did sometimes when he knew I needed it.

Yeah, there, there mate. You're alright.

He had a friendly face and a MacGyver mullet, which comforted me.

I'm ok, I said a minute later. My nerves must've been still keyed up from the flight.

Oh yeah, he nodded. Bloody turbulence. I prefer a good ol' Harley Davidson myself.

I took two more hits off the brown bag. He extended his hand.

Name's Cameron.

Henri.

We shook hands.

Where you fly in from?

Chicago, I said.

Oh, you dig the blues? B.B. King? Muddy Waters?

Cameron knew a lot of blues musicians. He seemed to think I was *from* Chicago.

Say, mate, you need any guitar lessons?

I might, I said, feeling a little more like myself. Are you a shredder?

He laughed.

I'd probably get a C for shredding, he said, maybe a C+, but I can teach you the basics. Enough to put you on any stage you like.

He swigged from a blue can of 1664 beer.

I've been here for seven months off the books, he said. I do odd jobs, drywalling. For the past couple months, I've been looking after a woman who's dying of cancer. You need work?

Oh, I appreciate it, but I got a gig in the entertainment business.

Yeah? Do tell, mate.

Well, it's under wraps for now.

Alright, he said, but I'm intrigued.

He had a glint in his eye. We agreed to meet for guitar lessons in two days. He scribbled the name and address of a cybercafé on a napkin.

The owner there lets me do the lessons in a side office, he said. Low rate. Nice people here. You'll like it.

We shook hands again outside the café.

Thanks Cameron, for everything.

He waived his hand.

Aw, think nothing of it mate. See you soon.

***

Ambling back to my place, it poured, and I tossed my pants in the dryer like an idiot. Even when I found the mutilated bar napkin Cameron had given me, I didn't think it was a great loss. I remembered him saying something about the cybercafé being near the Oberkampf metro stop, so I figured I could just get off there and ask people to point me in the right direction. But I ended up asking hundreds of people, Is there a cybercafé around here?

Most of them rumpled their faces at me and did the French lip fart (which means I don't know / I don't care). Around dinner time, I reckoned the cybercafé was some fly-by-night operation because I couldn't find a trace of one in that area in the phonebook or on the internet.

Back at my studio, defeated, I threw open my French windows. The sun set behind those Hussmannian buildings, and I peered out into the city and thought of Cameron, the Good Samaritan who'd rescued me from death-by-panic-attack-oxygen-deprivation. He was out there somewhere, getting stood up by some ass in the entertainment business. Why did I have to say *entertainment business*?

My social life pretty much came to a stand-still during that first month in Paris, and I only saw

sights incidentally, because I spent most my waking hours practicing or traveling with PSG, or
hoofing it through Oberkampf looking for a
phantom cybercafé. Cameron even helped me
again, in absentia, because all the running around,
in addition to training with the team, whipped me
into world-class shape. By the end of July, I
branched out and poked my head into other cybercafés.

Are you the owner? I would say. Do you
know an Aussie with a MacGyver mullet named
Cameron? No? Ok, do you at least know of any
cybercafés in the eleventh *arrondissement*?

During my first post-match interview, after
a pre-season friendly on August 1st, I answered
their questions in French and said, Oh, one more
thing if I could.

I addressed the camera in English.

Cameron, contact me through PSG. I lost
your address, and I've been looking for you.

And then in French.

Anyone who knows an Australian man
named Cameron, he has a mullet--

The interviewer yanked away the microphone.

I'm afraid we have to leave it there, he said.
Midfielder Henri Sauvé, who helped PSG to a 3 - 1
pre-season victory here tonight at the Parc des
Princes.

August and September came and went in a

flash. Along with six hours of field time each day, PSG had a giant weight room with every workout contraption known to man. I tried them all and spent many hours on the leg press machine, probably because there was a video game hooked up to it where you could beat your previous score.

My playing time ticked up in each of the first ten matches; I went from getting five garbage minutes, to 20 minutes a match by the end of October. At the start of November, Coach Lugo put me in for a whole half. In my precious few spare hours in my apartment, I learned guitar chords from a songbook, all of them, even A minor 7 and F sus 2.

Cameron, if you're reading this, I'm sorry I never found you again. Champion wishes to you in your life.

***

Along with some shit, nighttime terrors and panicked calls to Ruth and my friends, bright spots also emerged that first year in Paris, like my developing skill and increased playing time. Overall though, year one in the major leagues was an even-keeled slog. Intense workouts and weightlifting nine hours a day, not as many parties as one might think. I fetched things and carried bags. Rookie initiation bullshit. My year's highlight involved flying back to Tiger Island for Hanukkah and New Year's to party with friends. Etienne cajoled Gregor, Joseph, David, and me to sit through a Noam Chomsky lecture at the island art gallery. The MIT professor spoke about the looming war in Iraq; each of us left that evening with copies of his books.

After the talk, my friends and I played *No Limit Texas Hold 'Em* poker around a green-felt pool table in the basement of Etienne and David's cozy two-bedroom chalet. Sounds of Bob Dylan's Bootlegs Volume One on vinyl washed against us while we sipped whisky-straight and discussed Iraq, women, Paris, money, soccer contracts, and the re-emergent economic straits of our own tiny commonwealth.

They say we're falling short again, Etienne said. Big time too, like before the stadium.

It's the stadium loan interest, Joseph said. Did you all hear about that report from that economist?

Oh yeah, I said while the others nodded.

Call, Gregor said.

He splashed a few chips in the pot.

The interest is bad, David said, but I feel like too we've had a lot of newcomers, which, you know, stretches the basic income pie and the money needed for the health services.

Joseph, originally from the Sudan, glanced at Gregor who was born in Cincinnati.

There you go, he said. Blame the immigrants.

No, no, no, David said, rouging. I'm not

101

even saying newcomers are a problem, but it's just math.

The pot's good, I said. Show 'em.

We turned over our cards. Etienne had a flush, and Joseph's pocket pair gave him three of a kind. I'd hit a straight flush on the flop.

You fucker, Etienne said.

I raked in the pile of chips. Stacking them, I said, People around here are getting older too. You know, rising health services and all that.

Etienne sipped his whisky and rolled it around on his tongue, nodding.

I read in *La GP* today, he said, unless the *Bourse Collective* gets another revenue stream, we've got enough for three, maybe four more years of basic income before reductions. Eight years before it totally dries up. And that wouldn't be just like, a small policy change. We're talking about *gutting* the character of this archipelago.

I wouldn't have got my contract without it, Joseph said, because I wouldn't've been able to train full-time.

Joseph had signed with F.C. Copenhagen the week before.

None of us could keep training, Etienne said, getting a little more riled up. And good for us and our imaginary team, but really, it's about the walk-away-power for workers.

We all reflected for a minute and tasted our drinks. I dealt two cards to each person around the table.

How short are we? Gregor said. The commonwealth, I mean.

Etienne scratched his chin before he scurried up the stairs.

Don't, I said with a pained expression, eager to keep the flow of the game going.

He returned in a flash with that day's *La GP* and read.

It says 45,752 full-time-resident adult cardholders eligible for basic income.

He scanned down the page.

They need 80 million dollars more a year into the *Bourse Collective* by 2006 to keep it solvent, he said.

Damn, I said. I feel like that's not much.

I looked at Gregor.

How much do you make a year?

He hissed air through his teeth and shook his head.

Ya know, David said, what if we're the answer?

The four of us squinted at him.

We should resurrect the team and monetize it a little better, he said. Why hasn't anyone suggested converting our squad into a syndicalist franchise, like that guy in Argentina said that one time? We could be an MLS team, but community and worker-owned, with all our net profits going towards basic income.

The room became still.

I'd even come out of retirement if that was the plan, he added with a shrug, tossing a few more chips in the pot.

We all exchanged glances before turning back to him. David might as well have just come up with $E = mc^2$.

Holy shit, said Gregor before calling David's raise.

We've got a stadium, Joseph said, growing enthusiastic. And we've got the talent.

Yeah, David said, I bet we could get close, or at least work our way up to 80 million a year for total team profit beyond costs, salaries, and all that.

We left that night lavishing David with praise, calling him a genius, but he grinned sheepishly and said, Give me a break. Someone was bound to think of this.

We ran the idea through the necessary channels - Coach Thomas, our teammates, the stadium committee, the surrounding neighborhood associations, and the General Assembly - and it was met with enthusiasm at each turn. We even reached out to some of our former antagonisers who said they would rather die than attend our matches, but they also said if our profits went to the *Bourse Collective*, they would stop protesting us. It seemed nobody wanted reductions, or especially collapse, of our basic income.

The 2004 Olympics in Greece, Coach

Thomas said in a team meeting at her and her partner's chalet, will be our way in, to skyrocket the valuation of our team.

Yes, I said with a bobbing clutched fist.

A log popped in the fireplace.

The next day, we enlisted Monsieur Lefebvre, a Parisian-born international lawyer and father to Etienne and David. After wrangling with his eldest sons in 1998 over the stadium, he'd mellowed so much he even volunteered to help us pro bono. 2003 greeted the archipelago with vicious snow and ice. Indoors, by the fire, we planted seeds for spring.

***

Back in Paris in February, I'd just ushered in my 20th year of life and was finding ways to become involved in the community, which helped mitigate my anxiety. I attended anti-war demonstrations, wrote letters to newspapers and magazines, and donated money to legal defense funds for people who'd been arrested in acts of civil disobedience. Talk of the war crackled in the air, everywhere. Our mediocre, sub .500 season at PSG wound down in April when Gregor called me at my apartment for what would be a momentous phone call.

I vented to him for a bit about my micromanaged, 24/7 grind and asked how Renée was.

She's good, Gregor said. Rowing every day. Studying a lot.

Ever since a picture of Renée Lefebvre fluttered out of Gregor's sock in Sao Paulo, during our 1999 trip, I suspected he might be in love her. We teased him at first, but I and even Renée's three brothers, Etienne, David, and young Roland, our newest edition to the team, praised the relationship. I liked Renée ever since she let me look off her math answers when we were in year one.

How 'bout you? Gregor said on the other end. How you been? Met any *Parisiennes*?

Shit, I said with a big ol' grin, I haven't been going out enough. And they're hard to meet, surrounded by tourists and people coming and going. They live cordoned off, in friend enclaves.

Yeah, you'll meet the right one someday. How's Anelka and Okocha? [Two of my teammates.]

I think Okocha's done after this year. Anelka's cool. Most the guys though, they treat football like a job. They play, grab the cash, and go home, or party but don't invite me. There's no joy. *Our* team plays with joy. Ya know?

I do, Gregor said. But keep your head up for now brother. It was the same my rookie year. They made me carry shit all summer. Still, hardly any of 'em really talk to me like a friend, or hang out. It's all business. Half of 'em have families.

Daddies, I said.

Total daddies.

That's why we need our own club, I said.

Hell yeah. I pester Papa L for news every time I see him.

Renée said in the distance, Have you not told him yet?

Tell me what?

Will you stop? Gregor said. I'm about to.

They wrestled with the phone, it sounded like.

I'm gonna tell him, Renée said.

Tell me what!

Ok, are you ready? Gregor said, clearer.

Yes. Ready for what?

I proposed a life union to Renée, and she said - Gregor drew it out for suspense - yes!

Whoa! Congratulations brother.

Marriage as the rest of the world knows it didn't exist on the islands. Adult inhabitants over 18 defined their relationships for themselves. The ideal was love. As far as ceremonies went, couples or more invited their friends to sing, eat delicious food, dance, and listen to stories about their relationship. We eschewed state-religious relationship frameworks and built usual marriage benefits into our social contract. What Gregor proposed to Renée was the closest thing we had to *'til death do us part*.

So, Gregor said, I know this doesn't even need to be a question, but would you be my *homme d'honneur* (best man) at the ceremony?

My face lit up, and I yelled into the phone.

This is the greatest honor of my life!

Being the *homme d'honneur* meant that I would get to tell several stories at the event and that I'd become sealed to Gregor and Renée until the end of time. In a way, it was like winning a championship.

Gregor put Renée on speaker with him.

Renée, did you hear I'm the *homme d'honneur*?

I did, she said, trying not to bust up. Congratulations!

Thank you! Ya know, I should be soaking up some congratulations. This ceremony's gonna be a pretty big day for me.

The three of us yucked it up for 30 minutes before Gregor got on by himself again. He said he had one last thing to say.

It's another bombshell, if you can handle it.

Of course, but let me just steady myself here on this credenza.

I cracked my neck side to side.

Ok, go ahead.

Ok, Gregor said. so I found my birth-parents.

You found them?

I mean, I found out who they are. I met my birth-mother seven months ago. I didn't tell anyone because-- I don't know why. I wanted to wait until I had all the pieces put together.

Damn, I said, surprised.

It's crazy, Gregor said, but I feel like my birth-father has been in the background of my life all along. Without him, you might even be dead.

CHAPTER SEVEN: The Ghost Dad Maneuver

At 16, Gregor discovered a photo in his parent's closet of a woman who bore a strong, uncanny resemblance to him. He'd known since eight he'd been adopted, but as for the identity of his birth-parents, the photo constituted the first break in the case. He never dreamed of asking Dennis and Maude about it. He feared seeming ungrateful and hurting their feelings. Written on the back of the photo were the words: *Sally Cobb, Coral Gables, 1985.* Gregor hid the photo inside a French-language copy of Hemingway's *The Old Man and the Sea* for four years. In October of 2002, a month before his 20th birthday, he thought of the picture again.

He used a website called switchboard.com, an American white pages, to search for Sally Cobb in Coral Gables. Seven were listed. He started calling Sally Cobbs unbeknownst to anyone, even me. The fifth Sally Cobb confirmed that she'd had a baby in 1982 who was adopted by the Heinrichs on Tiger Island. She invited him to Coral Gables. He slipped out of Chicago during a two-day break in the season and flew to Miami for a 24-hour stay.

During the clandestine autumn rendez-vous, Sally told Gregor his birth was the fruit of a rotten tryst between herself and a powerful Cincinnati doctor. When I heard about the meeting, I pictured Gregor and Sally Cobb, seated around a circular glass coffee table, supported by wicker, old photos and documents scattered about. A white curly-haired dog roamed the breezeway, yipping to be let inside.

This is your birth-father, Gregor, I imagined her saying. *The man on the left.*

But I don't know how it happened exactly, or the shape of her coffee table, or if she even had a coffee table or a dog. I know she said the doctor forced her to terminate the pregnancy or else. She fled the Queen City to find refuge with a far-flung cousin way up in Marquette, Michigan. She was convinced that no matter where she landed, the doctor would get his way. He hired people. Ukrainians, she said. Vicious ones. She even feared for the baby's life once it was born.

The Marquette cousins, according to Sally, had been to the archipelago numerous times and were family friends of the Heinrichs, a childless couple. Sally never had her name affixed to any commonwealth documents. As she recounted her story to Gregor, she said she picked Coral Gables on a whim.

It was warm and far from Cincinnati and sounded like a place where someone could start over, she reportedly said to him.

She rented a studio with some seed money

from relatives in 1983 and got a job selling ice creams on the beach. She'd been there ever since, she said.

By her timeline, she'd have been a shade over 20 when she became pregnant with Gregor; the Cincinnati doctor would have been in the thick of his 63rd year. Gregor said Sally Cobb showed him several photos of herself and the famous doctor, some at his office, and one at an outdoor cocktail party. In the summer of 2003, Gregor showed me the photo from the party. Sally and the doctor appear in black-tie formal wear, lounging in poolside deck chairs. Ken Griffey and Mike Vail of the Cincinnati Reds can be seen holding fancy spirits, chatting in the background. The photo could have blended with stills from the set of *The Love Boat*.

***

At the end of the call in April, when Gregor asked me to be his *homme d'honneur*, he told me about his meeting with Sally Cobb. She'd only just turned 42, he said. Then his voice turned as sober as I'd ever heard out of him. I detected a tinge of excitement too.

My birth father-- are you ready for this?
Yeah.
He's Doctor Henry Heimlich.
Three full Mississippi-length seconds of silence passed. I searched my brain, hard.
Of the maneuver?

Yeah. That's him.

Is there any connection, I said, with the similarity of the last names? (Heimlich, Heinrich)

I asked Sally that, Gregor said. It's a total co-incidence as far as anyone can tell.

Gregor recounted Sally's allegations, which didn't sound good, but he said he'd remain neutral until he gathered more evidence. He wanted to hear both sides and avoid jumping to the wrong conclusions. Like anyone, I think Gregor har-bored a desire to see his birth-father in a good light. And he might have even been a little se-duced by the celebrity of the maneuver.

When I was three, I nearly choked to death on a starlight mint at a pizza parlor near the har-bor. Gregor knew this story. I grabbed my throat and turned blue. My mother saw me and started the forceful upward and inward thrusts. Her hands, in the grip of a Hulk Hogan double-ax-handle, pulled up below my little sternum. As a teacher, she'd been trained in the ways of the ma-neuver. Silence spread to every corner of the parlor; some folks thought she was abusing me. A man stood up in the back and yelled, Unhand that child!

But on her fourth thrust, the whole restau-rant witnessed the mint rocket out of my drooling maw and slide 14 feet across the parlor's stained hardwood floor.

I'm going to reach out to him soon, Gregor

said before we ended the call. I'm just waiting for the right time.

***

At six in the morning the day of the ceremony, I hopped on my bicycle and ran errands all over the island. Etienne loaded up a dozen cases of cognac onto my rented golf cart at eight, and I drove those clanking bottles 18 kilometers from the harbor to Parc Rochelle Baré, the sight of the festivities. David, Roland, and I had 200 chairs set up by ten.

During the vows, I stood up there closest to Gregor and was flanked on my right by Renée's three brothers, all four of us *témoins* in tan suits with navy skinny ties. Gregor's bottom lip quivered on first sight of Renée and her fishtail braid of long blond hair.

Paul presided over a beautiful ceremony, complete with excerpted readings from Wittman and Neruda. When the time came for my speech, before the meal, it became apparent I might've misjudged the power of cognac.

Renée, I said into the mic, is the best coxswain this archipelago's ever seen, ever gonna see. And have you seen her work with children? She's like a real live child wizard. And Gregor, well, he's the Michael Jordan. We've known it since single digit ages. He can't lose.

I peeled off my suit jacket and put it on the chair behind me. My tie hung loose around my collar. I clawed it looser still and scanned faces in the crowd, most either hysterical or stunned. A couple hundred islanders had gathered for the occasion. Little Arthur, who'd delivered the ring, sat giggling up on Paul's shoulders.

I love you all, everybody here I love, but if any one of you - I pointed out at the crowd - if any of you messes with either a-them, *ooooooh weee*.

People seemed befuddled and offered a smattering of polite or uncomfortable laughter. Monsieur Lefebvre locked a death glare on me, shook his head slightly, and mouthed the word, No.

I steadied myself on the mic stand.

Hammer time, you know? I said. You mess with 'em it's gonna be hammer time.

My teammates, Gregor included, all had real tears streaming down their faces from laughing or trying to contain laughter. Renée was a terrific sport.

Here's the main thing I wanna say, I said. Someday, twenty-five years from now, I'll be in a seaside manor, purchased with proceeds from my fourth or fifth novel--

People all over busted up laughing at that, even me a little too. I stifled a burp with my wrist, then continued.

And the phone will ring. My son Harrington will answer it. He'll knock on the door of my study, and say, *Father, I'm sorry to disturb your work, but Gregor and Renée have rung. I'll ask him, What's the call regarding my dear boy? And he'll say, They call to announce their love bubble has reconstituted itself through a quarter-century of storms and sunshine, and that it remains unbreakable.*

My gaze drifted out towards Lake Michigan for a long five seconds while the hilarity of my friends subsided.

I don't wanna be on earth without 'em, I said. I love 'em, and they're the best people to be betrothed to one another, or you know, whatever we do here.

I placed the microphone back on the stand and hugged them both. To my surprise, those in attendance said *aww* before cheering uproariously. A soul band struck up. I wandered off and vomited behind a pine tree. It was one of the best days of my life.

***

Gregor and Renée passed a honeymoon-esque get-away on Ko Li Pe, an island off the southwestern coast of Thailand. In the first week of July 2003, two days after their return, Gregor played a match in Kansas City before catching a flight to Cincinnati. His taxi rolled up the driveway of an eleven-bedroom, Georgian brick colonial the following day at noon. He wrapped resolutely, and a home health-care worker with orange hair answered the door.

May I help you?

I'm here to see the doctor. I made an appointment with his assistant.

He's resting now, she said.

Henry Heimlich was 83 at the time.

Oh, Gregor said. I can try again this afternoon.

He headed back to the idling cab.

Three hours later, when he returned, she gave him the same routine.

What does your visit regard? I can pass a message along to the doctor if you'd like.

I need to see him about a birth, Gregor said. I scheduled an appointment.

Well, I'm sorry, but I never received anything about an appointment. It's very strange that the office would schedule an appointment *here*.

Can you just tell the doctor that Gregor Heinrich is here? I travelled a long way to meet with him.

She sighed.

Well, I'll have to see. He might still be resting.

You know what, Gregor said, I'll just tell him.

From there, Gregor sort of forced his way past her into the house. He checked rooms with the woman trailing behind, yelling and slapping his arm, and he eventually discovered Dr. Heimlich snoozing in a stately study upstairs. The doctor's lanky legs hung over the edge of a leather loveseat, Gregor told me.

The home health care worker's histrionics woke up the old fella.

What? Babcock?

The doctor squinted.

You're not Babcock, he said. Who are you?

Gregor flailed, explaining the nature of his visit, but the elder Heimlich didn't understand.

There's reason to believe you're my biological father, Gregor said. Do you know this woman?

He held up a picture of Sally Cobb. Heimlich turned to his assistant, a wounded, angry look on his face.

Doreen, is that *Sally*?

Gregor said the old codger fired daggers from his eyes.

That woman is a liar! She's been after my money for years!

Early in the tumult, Gregor surveyed the scene, he said: the orange-haired woman slapping his arm, telling him to *git-git-git*; the angry, baffled old man; the mahogany study, medical texts floor to ceiling. Old pictures and yellowed news clippings spilled from Gregor's envelope.

I'm just here to have a conversation, Gregor said. I'm trying to find out why--

The woman shouted into the receiver of a rotary phone.

Police, lickety-split!

Gregor was waiting on another taxi when

the police showed up. They cuffed him and dragged him down to the station. He spent six nights there and missed two matches, which gave the Chicago and Cincinnati gossip journalists ammo for weeks. Henry Heimlich dismissed all paternal allegations as the, quote, *poppycock dream of a confused young anarchist.*

Gregor wrote a public letter of apology to the home health care worker. He published it on his website and said she'd had every right to get upset and call the police. A strange man had entered the home without permission. He also wrote that he was mistaken about the paternity allegations, and as a result, Henry Heimlich agreed to drop the trespassing charges.

The fallout and embarrassment from the incident persisted though. The Fire brass suspended Gregor for three matches and fined him $20,000 for ungentlemanly conduct. His coach chewed him out for embarrassing the organization, and a rivalry developed between them. They snipped at each other in practice over tactical decisions. The coach was also a staunch Bush supporter and didn't appreciate Gregor signing anti-war petitions and discussing his politics with the media.

A subpar post-suspension return and a couple more shouting matches landed Gregor on the bench for the rest of July, which was a scandal in the little world of MLS. He was the league's leading scorer up to that point. After the Cincinnati incident, instead of capturing his goals, the camera would pan to him occasionally while he defiantly spit sunflower seeds from his spot on the bench. The opposing team's fans taunted him with signs that said, *Heinrich, who's your daddy?*

Amid the turmoil, Renée, who'd been dividing her time between the island and Chicago, stayed with him for an extended visit. His morale inched upward, but then, the elder Heimlich's son, Peter, kept trying to recruit him for an anti-Dr. Heimlich crusade. In a gabardine suit, the 50-something Peter kneeled before Gregor and Renée at a table at the Chicago Diner's Halstead location. It was the fourth time Peter had approached him.

Look, Peter said, I don't know if we're brothers, but my father is a fraud. You have social clout, with your profession. We could team up to stop him.

Peter shared damning evidence from a variety of sources and claimed virtually all the elder Heimlich's post-maneuver research had been harmful. He alleged the doctor had injected HIV patients with malaria-infected blood in the hopes it would cure them. Peter said, with dubious results, some forged, that Dr. Heimlich had bilked thousands out of Jack Nicolson and Ron Howard to keep the scheme going.

Gregor asked Peter about Sally Cobb, and

he said that he couldn't confirm Sally Cobb's account. Peter did however allege that when he was nine, Dr. Heimlich once snatched a paddle ball from him and beat his ass with it. Gregor packed up Peter's documents in a folder.

Can you give me 72 hours with this stuff?

Of course, Peter said. Contact me as soon as you're ready, and together, we'll take down the treachery and lies of my father.

When Gregor and Renée returned home that night, Gregor drafted a letter: *I hereby tender my resignation from the Chicago Fire with immediate effect.*

***

When Gregor stepped off the ferry at the island harbor, he collapsed in my arms. My fingers combed his lush, sandy hair, some of it mixing into my jet-black raven feathers. Renée patted his back while he hung there on me.

I'm a joke, he said.

A small colony of white gulls circled overhead. We used to call them harbor vultures.

Hell no, I said. You ain't no joke.

I'd never seen him fly so low. But it didn't last long. A few seconds later, he broke from our embrace, and his posture straightened. He sniffed hard and wiped his nose.

You know what? He said. We can deal with it.

Yeah, I said. We're brothers and sisters.

Gregor cast his gaze to the harbor, the dusk

light slowly vanishing off the island coast. Renée put her arm around him.

Yup, he said. It's all our generation now.

The three of us listened to lake sounds for a few seconds. Gregor stayed staring out towards the water, and Renée glanced over at me.

You all should play ball tomorrow, she said with a wink.

Oh yeah, I said, that's the ticket. As soon as I get home, I'm calling Paul, Joseph, David, Ezra, and whoever else is still here. Tomorrow at daybreak, Rochelle Baré. Barefoot glory days round two.

I waited for a second.

I'd be down, Gregor said softly.

Renée grinned big, turning away. She knew him too well.

Back at my chalet that night, I dialed up all my teammates, but I made one more call, to Paris. It was 7:30AM there.

Allô?

Coach Lugo, I hope I'm not waking you.

Been up for two hours, he snapped. What can I do for you? Don't tell me you're coming in late from vacation.

No, I'm--

Is this about your anxiety problem? You've gotta meditate more, I'm telling you. You've got a big role to play in the mid-field now that Jay-Jay's [Okocha] out [transferred to Bolton].

123

No, I said. I'll be right on schedule. But what if I told you there's a superstar forward, a natural goal-scorer, who'd come to Paris before the start of the season.

Not interested, Lugo said with no hesitation.

Ok, but hear me out. You always say that finishing is our Achilles heel and--

Then put the ball in the goal, he said exploding with laughter.

I gave a courtesy chuckle.

I will, I said, but this guy, I know him. He'd boost our morale, and I guarantee he'd net 40 goals in his first season with us. We'd rise from the middle--

40? Who is he?

My brother, Gregor.

Gregor Heinrich? The answer's definitely no.

Why?

Sparring with the Chicago manager, Lugo said. Breaking his contract. Too many red flags.

But that coach is a jerk. He's a big Republican who hates our commonwealth. He's a Bush supporter.

Bush supporter?

Lugo hated Bush, like everyone in Europe.

Yeah, I said. Huge neocon donor. And if Gregor were to bolt from PSG, you could void my contract. I'd play for free. I'd bet my life on him succeeding here.

There was silence on the under end.

Hello?

So you think ol' Gregor could light it up for us?

I guarantee you he could.

Tell him (Lugo paused) I'll give him a run, a try out, if he'd be willing to do a one-year for a quarter million, or thereabouts.

I'll ring him right now, I said.

After Gregor netted a hat-trick in his PSG debut, Coach Lugo slapped me on the back a little too hard and said, I think ol' Gregor's gonna be a good friend of ours.

Henri Sauvé
From an Undisclosed Location
Wednesday, November 9, 2011

CHAPTER EIGHT: Our Paris

My inner-circle rented the Lux Bar in Montmartre for a Hanukkah blowout that's been etched in my brain's highlight reel ever since. The whole Tiger Island squad had arrived in Paris the day before because on Sunday, we'd play our comeback match: a friendly against the U-23 version of *Les Bleus* in the Stade de France. The timing was perfect too, because my head had never felt better. The last time I'd had a false-alarm meltdown was back in September.

Bolstering my upward crest, a baker's dozen from the island, friends not on the team, flew in to attend the party and watch us play. Ruth brought Arthur, who stayed back at the hotel that night, sleeping under the eye of a sitter. Friends I'd made in Paris over the past year-and-a-half mingled with friends of mine from my paste-eating days on the archipelago. Worlds collided, and I loved every minute of it.

The party quieted down at 10:30 for the readings. Jules treated us to an E. K. McNamara poem about Anne Frank. Ruth said the Hebrew and lit the menorah, which caused me to mist but not cry.

We fit so many people, around 60, into the

tiny joint. We sipped Manhattans, told tall tales, argued politics, teased each other, and laughed and laughed and laughed.

Lucas and I booked the midnight mystery musical guest, Matt Sharp. We expected him solo, but he showed up with two of his bandmates from The Rentals: Maya Rudolph, who was also an actor on *Saturday Night Live*, and Petra Hayden. A guy, just a regular-looking bloke, lugged gear for them. He helped the band and a couple bar staff members set up before milling around in the back. I brought him a Manhattan and extended my hand.

I'm Henri. Manhattan?

That's mighty kind of you, Henri.

He took the drink and shook my hand.

Paul, he said.

Do you play with the Rentals?

No, I'm just along for the ride.

Do you play music?

I'm afraid I don't.

He tasted the drink, and I searched for something else to say.

Man, have you ever heard of *The Book of Lists*?

Paul searched his memory.

The one by the Wallaces and the Wallechinsky, I said. It's from the '70s.

Yeah, he said slowly, with a look of recognition. Is that the one with a list about Deaths from

Strange Causes?

I pointed excitedly.

That's the one.

Yeah, he said. I remember one from that list about a guy choking to death on a toothpick.

I grinned ear to ear, a little toasty on my third drink.

And the one, Paul said, about a Greek painter, from whatever B.C., who laughed so hard at his own painting of an old hag that he broke a blood vessel in his brain and died.

We busted up laughing.

Poor bastard, I said. That's gotta be a helluva funny painting though. Do you remember the list of ghost sightings?

After hobnobbing with Paul, I rejoined my friends near the Rentals trio. They played two longer ambient songs interspersed with five Rentals songs. She Says It's Alright from their second album blew up into a full-bar sing along. White holiday lights adorned their tall chairs and the floor around them in the dark room. Their music struck the perfect note. No one yelled Free Bird or asked Matt questions about Weezer the entire night.

Gregor and I congratulated Maya and Petra on a fantastic set while Matt packed up. We talked about when they played on Tiger Island once, in the theatre next to the art gallery. Matt came over, and their roadie, Paul, navigated the packed house to join us moments later.

Have you two met my partner Paul? Maya said to Gregor and me.

No. Hi Paul. I'm Gregor.

They shook hands. Even though I had a huge crush on Maya, I couldn't muster any animosity for Paul. He seemed like a genuinely cool and decent feller.

We've met, I said, gesturing to Paul.

Henri and I go way back, Paul said, to light chuckles.

At some point, the bartenders and staff amalgamated into the party. Lucas had assembled a dance party mix-tape for the occasion, and everyone in the joint cut a rug and belted out the lyrics to Crocodile Rock, Dancing with Myself, and Rebel Rebel until 4AM Saturday. Lux Bar hit it out of the park so hard we added another 20% to our final tab. And just when I couldn't imagine that night becoming any more legendary, I damn near caught the Holy Ghost the next day when Etienne furnished me with conclusive evidence that I'd been sipping Manhattans and chatting about *The Book of Lists* with fucking Paul Thomas Anderson.

***

Coach Thomas rarely yelled at us out of anger, instead taking the stoic approach to team management. But we moved so sluggish in our light workout in the Parc des Princes Saturday evening that we forced her hand.

Do you have any idea who we're facing tomorrow! This is our chance to bury the memory of 10 - 0, but you've got me worried it might happen again!

We lucked out that the match kicked off at 8:00PM on Sunday, putting 40 hours between us and the party, because we needed a championship performance. This match carried the potential to raise our profile and help our MLS bid. All week, the media buzz was hot and heavy, which is rare for a matchup of U-23 teams. Much of the coverage discussed how Gregor and I, along with Lucas and our newest island teammate Timothée Vars, both of whom signed with PSG shortly after Gregor, helped lead the French club to its best start since its founding in 1970: 14 wins, five ties, and no losses. Our anti-war activism and the archipelago's historical connection to France only added to the special aura swirling around the match.

***

Hints of snow eddied in the lights above 60 thousand cheering spectators in the Stade de France. We got moving on the pitch and steam poured from our young heads. Gregor and I yanked small tufts of grass from the pitch during warm ups and stuffed them in a plastic baggie. We planned to transport the green blades back to Tiger Island and sprinkle them in with some weed in a joint. It was the hallowed ground where, as youngsters agitating for our own stadium, we watched *Les Bleus* triumph on world football's biggest stage. We wanted to internalize the place.

I tossed the baggie in my duffle and ran up to each of my teammates and put my forehead to theirs.

You ready for this shit? I said into every pair of eyes on the touch line. After tonight, the world's gonna know we're back.

The ref called for captains, and Coach Thomas whipped around to all of us on the bench.

Did you all vote on a captain yet?

She shivered in her giant parka.

No, several of us said.

She pointed at our new starting goalkeeper.

Ezra, you wanna be captain tonight?

He stood up, 6' 4" and a month from 20.

Sure, he said.

Coach Thomas knew that Ezra's parents, Ethiopian Jews who'd opted for Tiger Island (instead of Israel) after Operation Moses in the 1980s, had made the trip all the way from the archipelago to see their son play. He'd bloomed in such a big way after the 2000 Olympics, once he found his confidence. He never stopped training and improving.

After Ezra won the coin toss and elected for us to kick off, we sprung out of the gate like stallions with ESP. Three of our shots whizzed past the French post in the first 10 minutes. Jupiter Agoot, another up-and-comer who'd arrived from the Sudan in '89 with Joseph's cohort, locked it down for us in the back. He and his mates in defense - Timothée, Paul, and David - only let Ezra see two lousy shots in the first half. The score remained 0 - 0 until the 48th minute.

Timothée hit me with a leading pass near mid-field. I caught up to it and dribbled ten or twelve yards into their territory. Coach Thomas cupped her hands over her mouth and sent him.

Timothée, make the run!

Timothée blasted off up field. I passed it to Gregor ahead of me, and Gregor fed me back. Timothée had timed his run to perfection when I put the ball up. He needed only one touch before he wound up. The shot was quite a cracker, and a special one for Timothée, a Paris-native turned commonwealth cardholder in late 2000, narrowly missing the chance to play on our first Olympic squad.

There you go husky man, I said to him, squeezing his arm as we jogged back to our kick-off spots after a brief celebration.

Timothée grinned ear-to-ear.

Yeah baby, he said, one for the hometown crowd.

Gregor added a toe-poke beauty with two French defenders hanging on him to give us a 2 -

133

0 advantage in the 77th minute. Victory seemed all but certain until the ref called a controversial hand ball in the box on David. Franck Ribery buried the penalty for France. After nine tense minutes of sloppy boom ball, plus four extra-long minutes of stoppage time, the ref blew three extended whistles and waved his hands over his head. Ray Hudson called the match for ESPN radio: *Who on earth would have predicted it? The island boys are back, this time with a lightning bolt from the football gods!*

Something good had happened that night. Two months later it would become monumental.

***

The wave of goodness following the Hanukkah party and our big upset swept me into 2004. In February, Gregor, Lucas, Timothée, and I left Paris to reunite with the island squad in Guadalajara, Mexico. Our mission: qualify for the 2004 Olympic tournament in Greece. First order of business: vote for a team captain.

In the hotel lobby, with all 15 of us gathered around a couple wicker sofas in our black and red warm-up suits, Gregor raised his hand and surprised even me. He asked Coach Thomas if he could say something first.

The floor is yours, Coach Thomas said.

Thanks, Coach. I just wanted to say, we all saw how Henri got us fired up before our match at the Stade de France, and how he played unselfishly and got a nice assist that night. He's done that type of thing for us before. Lifting us up when our spirits might've been down. For those reasons, I'm nominating him for captain.

I pretended to hide my face in my track jacket.

David jumped in.

Yeah, I'll second that.

Third, Joseph said.

Ok, Coach Thomas said. Any other nominations or discussion?

She looked around.

Nobody? Does anyone oppose Henri being named captain? Etienne? Jupiter?

Nope, Jupiter said.

Etienne gave a thumb up. No one else said anything.

Coach Thomas stepped towards me. I was sitting on the couch in between Ezra and Jules' younger brother, Eric. My eyes rose to meet hers, and I thought of my meltdown phone call to her on my first visit to Paris.

Now what I'm about to say, Coach Thomas said, might surprise some people.

Everyone sat still and quiet, waiting. Especially me.

This kid, she continued, who used to have long bangs (à la Eddie Furlong circa *Terminator 2*) flapping in his face and would cut his hair only for the occasional Mohawk; the kid who nearly got us all arrested in Brisbane for hitting a cop in the leg with a bouncy ball; this kid grew up. He shaved all his hair off, persevered through some hard knocks, and now, [Coach Thomas extended her hand.] he's our team captain.

I sprung up from my seat and hugged her. My teammates clapped and whooped.

We can go all the way, she said in my ear, but I'm gonna need your help. Are you up for it?

I pulled back from our embrace and looked her in the eye.

One thousand percent, I said.

I think I might be interrupting a tender moment, Monsieur Lefebvre said, strolling into the lobby.

We all craned our necks towards him. Gregor clapped his palms together and said, Daddy's home, daddy's home, daddy's home.

We all busted up laughing except for David who heartily rolled his eyes.

What's up, Monsieur L? Joseph said. You made the trip down to watch us?

I'm here to watch, he said, and deliver news from my meeting with the MLS brass in New York City.

All ears perked up and a seriousness settled over us. Monsieur Lefebvre set his briefcase on the arm of one of the couches and produced two separate paper-clipped piles of documents.

So, he said with a pair of reading glasses perched on the bridge of his nose, I've got some good news and bad news.

Bad news first, Lucas said.

Ok, the bad news. We've been muscled out of the MLS *markets under consideration*.

That didn't sound good. I scanned the room, not sure whether I should be gnashing my teeth and pulling out my hair.

So? Etienne said.

So, Monsieur Lefebvre said, there's gonna be two expansion teams added to MLS for the season beginning April 2005, named on September 2nd of this year. Atlanta, San Diego, Cleveland, Nashville, Baltimore, and Miami are top in the running.

What's the good news? I said with desperation.

Ah ha, he said, I knew *you* wouldn't forget. The good news is you still have a slim chance to be one of the two expansion franchises.

How? Gregor said. How slim?

Coach Thomas looked on intently with her arms crossed.

Because of your big win against France, Monsieur Lefebvre said, and the media reaction and surprise that a team from an archipelago of 92,000 can beat a top team from a country of 65 million, I argued that once you win gold in Greece, your market value would be so high that they couldn't afford to pass up your bid.

Win gold? I said. What'd they say?

Oh, they laughed their heads off. Don Garber, the MLS boss said, *After losing 10 goals to 0 in that nightmare match against Italy, if they make it to the knockout stage, I'd be impressed.* So I asked him, *Impressed enough for the team bid?* He said, *Not quite, but I'll tell you what: if those boys win gold, we'll ratify your team bid with the management structure you outlined.* So I said, *I'll have my paralegal draw up a* contract under suspensive condition.

And? I and a few of my teammates said, leaning forward.

Monsieur Lefebvre shuffled in his brief case and pulled out a single document.

They call Garber *The Soccer Don,* he said.

With a sly grin, Monsieur Lefebvre held up the paper and pointed to some chicken scratch near the bottom.

That's what his signature looks like.

Henri Sauvé
From an Undisclosed Location
Thursday, November 10, 2011

CHAPTER NINE: Stuck Dreams Melt
On Tiger Island in June of 2004, Coach
Thomas reserved the media room of the indoor
activity center so we could all watch the seeding
for the Olympic tournament on ESPN 2. They
had a movie projector in there. We later cajoled
her into extending our reservation by two hours
because the idea got stuck in our heads that nothing would be better than a screening of *The Bourne
Identity* with root beer floats. I volunteered to pick
up the ice cream because no one else did, and because I knew I'd get to drive one of the activity
center's biodiesel golf carts. There were no cars on
our islands, and I admit, I enjoyed slamming the
petal to the floor, even if the vehicle topped out at
a whopping 25 kilometers per hour.
The creamery was near the island's eastern
shore, in between the Gallerie de l'Ile and the university district. I stomped the cart's parking brake
into place and hopped out. The little bells jingled
on the door when I walked in. The place used to
be a woodworking building, up until four years
before, and it still had a primitive, rustic feel. Two
separate families with children and a group of
teenagers ate ice cream and chatted on long
wooden benches scooted up to dining tables. Tu

Peux Pas Savoir, a 1960s yéyé pop song by Ria Bartok, set the upbeat soundtrack. After I strolled up to the counter, one of the teenagers hushed his voice only slightly and informed his four friends, That's Henri Sauvé, the soccer player.

Is anyone working here, I hollered into the back, or can I just help myself?

The latch popped open on the door of a steel, industrial freezer. Barney tumbled out, the frosty air nipping at his back. He was in his late fifties, an American who'd emigrated here to escape Vietnam. He and my father got paired together five years in a row during their annual weekend of volunteer maintenance duty on visitor housing, and my father invited him, his wife, and his young daughter over for dinner once when I was twelve.

Bonsoir Barn, I said.

He grinned and replied in English.

Henri. You here for the team pickup?

Yeah. Should be six of the large boxes of vanilla.

He lifted a clipboard from a nail on the wall and checked the orders.

Yep, just packed 'em up an hour ago.

He put the clipboard back and made for the freezer but hesitated.

Oh, before I forget, have you seen this?

He rummaged through stuff on a desk around the corner and tossed an Arabic language newspaper on the counter in front of me.

A friend of mine who's in Lebanon sent that to me, he said. Check out page seven.

He disappeared into the cooler while I flipped through the paper, *Al Amal*. I couldn't read any of the script but recognized the photo of the Iraqi National Orchestra playing in our stadium, all in dresses and tuxedos. They'd performed at half-time of our friendly match against Iraq three weeks before. Instead of a half-time team talk, we all went on the pitch and sat in the grass, side-by-side the Iraqi players who were already out there listening. I hoisted little Arthur over the barrier after spotting Ruth in the crowd and brought him and his toy lightsaber with me on the pitch to hear the music. Lower down the paper, there was an action photo of me, Jupiter, and an Iraqi player vying for the ball.

It says you guys are the Great Satan, Barney said.

I glanced up to see him wheeling a hand truck stacked with ice cream.

I'm just kidding ya, he said smirking. That was a special night, wasn't it? Our whole stock was bought out. We had a line two kilometers long. It was all-hands-on-deck.

Did you get to see the match?

Barney parked the load of ice cream.

Oh yeah. I was there with my daughter. Got a call on my cell phone that the place was blitzed and hustled here after.

141

He eyeballed the two families and the group of teens there and lowered his voice, seemingly ready to lay some top-secret truth on me.

So, you guys think you can pull this off? Winning gold, launching a pro team, saving the goddamn basic income?

Well, if--

Because when I first got here, I was AWOL. *Mỹ Lai* happened during my first tour. Was home for ten days before my second tour, and I said, *No way I'm going back with those butchers.* But there's no statute of limitations on desertion, you know? It's different than just draft dodging.

Dang, I said, mustering surprise even though I'd heard the story.

How old're you, Henri?

I snuck a quick peek at the ice cream behind him.

21.

See, I was two years *younger* than you are now. I came here with nothing, spoke no French, knew I probably wasn't ever gonna get to go back to Michigan to see my friends. And I haven't been back in 35 years. That's a big decision to make when you're 19, you know? I'da been dead in the water without that basic income cash, eating out of a garbage can for real, especially in my early 20s when I was a wreck, you know, mentally.

I nodded.

Hell, he said, we couldn't've launched this

creamery, my six friends and me, without basic income, for the startup capital. I know that for damn sure.

I hope we can help keep it going, I said.

Barney smacked his lips in faux-disappointment and ribbed me with a smile.

C'mon man, you *hope*?

With his voice lower still, he said, You and I are kind of alike. I know you lost your parents young, but I didn't have anyone in the generation above me neither, when I was your age. They were all against us.

Barney put his hand over his chest.

Now, my folks weren't dead, so I'm not saying it's entirely the same, but we stopped speaking and I never saw 'em again. When my daddy went to his grave, I hadn't seen 'im in-person in 29 years. 33 years with my momma, when she passed. So I'munna tell you something real quick cuz you might not be hearing it, but you need to.

He looked me square in the eye. I was slightly annoyed. I didn't wanna talk about dead parents, I just wanted to hurry up and go. And by all indicators, he'd been hitting his own stock pretty hard. Waffle cone crumbs dangled in his beard, and I smelled chocolate ice cream on his breath.

It's your time, Barney said in a whisper. Maybe it's coming early, cuz you're jus a young pup, but believe me, you'll make your life's legacy

over there in Greece. And I can tell you from experience, when the going gets tough, there ain't
gonna be no cavalry or daddy swooping down.
Jus you and your friends around you. So rely on
each other, but be ready to step the fuck up.

I listened, becoming more like the ice
cream behind us. By that I mean softening a little.

I will, I said. We're ready.

There you go, he said becoming louder
and more jovial again. Make it count, my man.

Barney tilted back the hand truck and
wheeled it around the counter before slapping me
on the back.

It ain't soft-serve, he said with a big grin, but
it is *self*-serve.

***

Once I loaded up the boxes, I punched the
go-pedal and strategized my route. I'd come by
way of the cart-path up by the stadium, but I decided to cut through the wooded area on the
northeast edge of the residential district to save
some time. I was already running a few minutes
behind. Under the old oak trees, my cart fishtailed
on a mud slick - I'd slept through racks and racks
of rain falling on the island that morning - and my
front tires spun idle. I hit the pedal again. Reverse.
Forward. Reverse. Stuck.

Merde.

I laid my head on the steering wheel and
contemplated my recent inability to seal the deal.

After tearing through the qualifying tournament in Guadalajara, we lost in the final because I got caught up too far; the USA burnt us for a transition goal, topping us 2 -1. Worst of all though was the disastrous conclusion of our otherwise stellar season at PSG.

In a penalty shootout for the finals of the Coupe de la Ligue, Gregor stepped to the spot. The crowd in Lyon had been ruthless, chanting and hollering, *Alors, c'est qui ton papa?* or some such French version of *Who's your daddy?* I'd buried my kick, and I rested down on my knee holding hands with Timothée and another teammate to my other side.

C'mon brother, I whispered over and over. Put it away.

When the keeper guessed correctly and stopped it, the crowd went ballistic. Gregor stood there, frozen with his hands on his hips. I went out to console him, but he seethed with such rage that I wondered if I'd get zapped or something if I touched him. They converted their next kick to clinch the title.

We faced Lyon again in May, in the final of the Coupe de France in Paris. With 75,000 packed into the Stade de France, in the waning minutes, the score held at 1 - 1. The match seemed destined for penalties again. I marked Sylvian Wiltord at the inside right edge of our box, but he stopped in front of me so abruptly that I bumped him, toppling him over. I'd had my eyes on the pass bending towards us. After he tumbled to the ground, and the ref blew his whistle, my heart stopped.

No, no, no, no, no, no, I begged.

Wiltord sank the penalty kick he'd been awarded and that was that. Lyon again, 2 - 1. After the match, at the stool in front of my locker, neither Gregor nor I spoke, but I felt judgment in his eyes.

You know what, I said, I made my [penalty] kick [last game], but I fucked it up tonight. So, sorry everyone.

I didn't say anything, Gregor snapped, rising to his feet. Not everything's about you.

Back on the island, in the last of the vanishing dusk light, I lifted my head from the steering wheel of the golf cart and dialed him on my cell phone. No answer. Etienne. David. Joseph. Coach Thomas. Timothée. Every last one of them was glued to the selection show, I imagined. I was at the edge of the forest. The moon barely shone through the trees. My eyes adjusted in the dark, enough to notice the sunken tops of the ice cream boxes. I threw the cart in neutral, hopped out, and shoved with my shoulder. The ol' girl was steadfast.

I scavenged around for a minute and found a decent-sized fallen branch as tall as I was. I snapped off its side-branches. It was long enough to sneak above the boxes to the go-pedal, so I pushed the cart and pressed the pedal with the branch at the same time. The front wheels just spun though, spitting mud on my legs.

I paced around for a second and contemplated leaving the cart and running with as much ice cream as I could carry, but I estimated I was still about five kilometers from the activity center. I tilted my head down at my pristine, official Tiger Island team track jacket and groaned. My fingers ran across its embroidered crest.

Aww, I said, nice knowing you buddy.

I wedged the jacket in front of the left tire before peeling off my t-shirt and stuffing it underneath the right one. In position, with the stick on the pedal, I heaved the cart loose, falling to my knee with the final shove. Mud caked up my left leg and forearm. I gathered my soiled clothes and gunned it, bound for the paved path I should've been on all along. As soon as I reached it, my phone buzzed. David. I didn't answer. Etienne called next. I yelled out into the night.

I'm coming!

The cart's tires skidded to a stop in front of the activity center. After locking the emergency brake and leaping out, I scooped up three of the boxes and hustled inside to the freezer, but the kitchen door was locked. I booked it to the media room, also locked. But I could see inside. The screen glowed in the dark. Some girlfriends, a boyfriend, some friends, and a few parents along with my whole team gathered 'round the show. Their faces looked serious. Grave even.

Let me in!

Nobody moved. They were all transfixed. With a big box of ice cream under each arm, I head butted the door twice.

Somebody!

Coach Thomas caught sight of me and got up. She pulled open the door handle, her eyes still fixed on the projected images. I walked in. Nobody seemed to notice. I looked up at what had them all so mesmerized. Two ESPN 2 analysts in suits around a studio desk discussed our plight.

I'm just not sure I see a way through for Tiger Island, the one in the blue suit said. *They might be the favorite in their first match against Costa Rica, and even there not by much, but then they face England, a powerhouse team who's been red hot. And then they finish up the group stage against Italy who, how could anyone forget, trounced them in Australia 10 - 0.*

Black suit cut in.

And we have to consider the pillars of that team, Gregor Heinrich and Henri Sauvé, haven't fared well recently in big, pressure-cooker matches for their club side, PSG.

Well, blue suit said, *we know artists flock to Paris, but after those PSG finals loses, members of the French media are saying that apparently, that's even true for choke artists.*

Ouch, black suit said while they both chuckled. *They're gonna have to turn things around if they wanna avoid another early exit from the Olympic tournament.* [Cheesy music struck up.] *And when we come back, our pre-Olympic coverage continues with...*

My forehead glistened with frustrated sweat under the glow of a Nike commercial. Vanilla ice cream dripped from the corners of the boxes and speckled my muddy legs and shoes. I couldn't believe it. We'd drawn the group of death.

Where have *you* been? Gregor said, his curiosity mingled with agitation.

I gulped air, unsure how to best answer the question.

And your shirt! David laughed.

I wasn't wearing one. All at once, thirty-some sets of eyes landed on me.

Ok, I piped up loudly, who has a key to the goddamn freezer?

Everyone shrugged and looked at the person next to them. Etienne helped me track one down, but after ten minutes, we discovered it was on the key ring for the golf cart, in my pocket the whole time.

Henri Sauvé
From an Undisclosed Location
Friday, November 11, 2011

CHAPTER TEN: Living in the Group of Death
The sun shimmered on the Gulf of Patras at noon. Etienne, David, Jules, Ezra, and I sat with Jupiter around a small, circular table at a beachside café. The sound of waves crashing and children building sandcastles relaxed me after filling up on Quinoa salad and Spanakopita. Etienne caught a glimpse of Joseph power walking up to our table with a newspaper in his hand; he sported wayfarer sunglasses and a t-shirt with *Made in Sudan* written across it. All five of us turned towards him. He flopped down that day's edition of *The New York Times*.

Check this, Joseph said, opening the paper to the Sports section. We got some ink.

On the bottom half of the front page was a picture of Lucas, having netted the first goal of his international career, celebrating with Gregor and Joseph. Gregor had dropped Lucas a ball thirty yards from the goal, and Lucas struck a one-touch floater that sailed over the Costa Rican keeper.

Above the riotous photo, the headline read:

Page D-1
August 10, 2004

At Olympics, Tiger Island Picks Up Where It Left Off

by JODI KITSANTONIS

ATHENS, Greece

The Tiger Island men's soccer team won its opening match at the Olympic Games, 3 - 1, against Costa Rica on Wednesday at a sold out Pampeloponnisiako Stadium in Patras.

The game was deadlocked at 0 - 0 until the 52-minute mark when Costa Rican striker Álvaro Saborío capitalized on a free kick from 22 yards out, which came as the result of a late tackle by Tiger Island's newly minted captain, Henri Sauvé.

Tiger Island, however, roared back with three goals, each coming in ten minute successions. At 61 minutes, star striker Gregor Heinrich evened the match, before assisting substitute Lucas Dujardin at 71; Sauvé, making good on his earlier mistake, assisted defender Timothée Vars, who scored in the 81st minute after streaking goalward from his position on the other side of the pitch.

The victory secures three points for the team from the 92,000-inhabitant North American commonwealth, who currently sit atop one of

152

the most fearsome four-somes in the men's Olympic soccer tournament.

Tiger Island face England on Saturday, and finish the group stage on August 17th with a match against tournament favorite Italy, who defeated them in spectacular fashion, 10 - 0, at the 2000 Olympic Games in Australia.

Despite the looming memory, the coach and architect of the Tiger Island team, Abeba Thomas-Dupont, emphasized how far her young squad has come since then.

"In the past year, we've tallied wins against [the U-23 teams of] France and Spain, and almost half of our team plays professionally in Europe and in the US," Thomas-Dupont, a Martinique-born former striker for Montpellier HSC in France, said in a post-game press conference Wednesday. When asked about the reasons behind her team's upswing, she cited maturation and commented, "Coming from a small archipelago that's cold most of the year, we tend to be close-knit. We've got this incredible team dynamic, like a family, which I think has translated to success on the pitch."

Over half of the players on Tiger Island's roster, remarkably, are linked to at least one other teammate through familial connections. Heinrich, the team's leading scorer, is married to the sister of Etienne, David, and Roland Lefebvre, brothers and teammates all, and Sauvé was adopted at age 15 by Heinrich's family. Midfielders Jules and Eric Solomon, like the Lefebvre's, are biological brother-teammates, and almost all others on the team have been playing as a unit on the syndicalist archipelago in Lake Michigan since childhood.

That is when Thomas-Dupont, in 1997, shepherded the team under her tutelage and began to cultivate its slash-and-burn playing style, which involves lightening quick one-touch passing and surprise sprints up the field by defenders and midfielders hoping to create scoring chances.

Thomas-Dupont hopes her emergent squad will convert enough of those chances to continue a path she views as having begun four years ago.

She told reporters, "When I remember [the 2000 Olympics in] Sydney, I don't dwell on the 10 - 0 loss. I think more of our resilience, coming back from two tough losses to defeat a very skilled Czech Republic team. In a way, with our win today, it feels like we're picking up where we left off."

***

Ezra had such long arms. He could have hugged King Kong Bundy and still clapped his hands together on the other side. And once he learned how to position himself, and catch the ball like it was magnetized to his gloves, his reach and ability covered a preponderance of the goal.

Several times in practice, when he robbed me of shots that seemed destined to go in, I'd shake my fist and say, *Zut alors*, Ezra!

I was just glad we were on the same team, and I didn't have to face him in match play.

Ezra signed his first professional contract in July of 2004. After the Olympics, he'd be headed to Belgium to join Standard Liège. But even with all the strides Ezra made, just like anyone on the team, especially me, he remained susceptible to the occasional poor decision on the pitch.

39 minutes into our second group stage match, Gregor tallied one of his visionary strikes off a give-and-go he put together with Joseph, and we led 1 - 0 going into half-time. The second half started, and I hung back with our defenders to protect the lead. The Brits created a couple chances for themselves, but around the eightieth minute, the 1 - 0 score remained intact. I felt a freak out coming on. We had the chance to advance out of the group of death outright, in our first two matches, and not even have to worry about Italy.

I wasn't the only giddy soul on the pitch either. David and Paul bounced up and down, clapping and grinning when the ball would go out of play. Anytime Timothée and Jupiter got near one of our teammates: copious backslapping and high fives. Joseph, after he put a shot just right of the crossbar, did a little shimmy that got a smile and an eye roll even from Coach Thomas.

Then in the 82nd minute, England caught us pushed up too far, for a split second, and they strung together a break away. We left poor Ezra to face a two-on-one against England's veteran captain, Michael Owen, and a scrappy, husky 18-year-old forward named Wayne Rooney. I crossed half field, sprinting, when Ezra dove on the pitch and grabbed Rooney's leg and pulled him down. Ezra punched the ball out of bounds for what would have been a corner kick, if there'd been no rules about grabbing the opponent's legs.

The Paraguayan ref brandished the red card in Ezra's face before Jupiter, Etienne, Gregor, and I'd even arrived to plead our case. Paul and Jules walked Ezra off, encouraging him arm-in-arm, and Coach Thomas greeted him at the touch-line while he undid his keeper gloves and sniffed, fighting tears. With the red card, he'd have to sit out the next match.

17-year-old Stanley Roth, a new recruit from the island, jogged out to our goal. He sported rec goggles like Horace Grant, though, as a 5-foot-8, 68-kilogram Jewish footballer, his specs were about the only thing he had in common with the former Chicago Bull. Lucas cheered him on from the bench.

C'mon, Stanley! You got it, man!

In his first international appearance, Stanley was greeted by a scorching penalty kick from Michael Owen. I reckon the ball would've knocked him back in the goal if he'd've even gotten a paw on it. Union Jacks and St. Georges' Crosses fluttered all over the raucous, sold out stadium. My soul floated twenty yards above the pitch, and I saw myself down there, ready to hurl.

David lowered his head in front me, trying to make eye contact.

Anybody home? This match isn't over.

He slapped my cheek.

Henri!

I looked at him.

We gotta tie them, David said. We need the point.

You're right.

I jogged over to the rest of the defense.

Everybody huddle up, I said. Stanley, that's the last time we let 'em score on you, ok? Shake it off. Nothing anybody coulda done. Jupiter, Paul, David, Timothée: Island Curtain time. Ten minutes, and we get out of here with a point.

We got this, Paul said.

Yeah, Jupiter said, bumping Stanley's keeper-gloved fist with his own. We got your back.

I jumped up and down before the kickoff to restart the match.

Allons-y les gars!

Jules cheesed and pointed to me from across the pitch.

I hear you Sauvé!

But with a one-man advantage, England picked us apart and scored five minutes later. We lost 2 - 1.

***

Stanley blubbered in the bathroom on the eve of our rematch with Italy. Roland Lefebvre, his roommate in our hotel in Athens, knocked on my door. I opened it, clad in my lucky blue beagle sweatshirt under a brown, vintage Arizona-quilted puffer vest. Shades with purple lenses rested on the bridge of my nose.

Can I help you, young Lefebvre?

Stanley won't leave the bathroom. He's been in there for an hour and a half.

I turned back to Etienne, Jupiter, Gregor, and David sitting around a small table covered in cards, poker chips, and glass bottles of the Greek version of Diet Squirt. Each held two cards and wore a poker face, except David who made a poor effort fighting his grin when he said, Do you think he might kill himself?

Roland huffed.

No, I don't think he's gonna kill himself, but he did say he was gonna leave.

What do you mean, *leave*? Etienne said from his spot at the table.

He said he was buying a plane ticket tomorrow, before the match. I think he wants to quit and go home.

My head tilted up toward the ceiling, and I looked back at my comrades, hoping for a suggestion.

You're the captain, Gregor said a tad bitchily.

I sauntered with Roland down to Stanley's room. Fire escape routes on the wall, written in five languages, caught my eye on the way. We were a long way from home.

I wrapped lightly on the bathroom door.

Stanley, this is Henri. Open up.

No noise.

Stanley, c'mon man.

David walked in a minute after me and cop-knocked.

Stanley, he said, you can open the door, or we can get Gregor and Jupiter to kick it down.

David cinched the belt of his gold-monogrammed hotel robe.

Or, he said, we can tell Coach Thomas you're having a nervous breakdown, and she can call the Greek authorities.

Facing David, my open wingspan and bulged eyes signified my displeasure with his unorthodox approach, but he just shrugged. A couple seconds later, we heard motion. The door clicked unlocked. I shooed David away and slipped inside. Stanley's eyes were red.

Hey man, I said, I know you're nervous

about the match.

I'm not playing in the match. I'm going home.

Fiston, you can't.

Stanley hoisted himself up on the marble bathroom counter.

I was in for ten minutes, and England scored two goals on me. If I play against Italy, I'll embarrass everyone and wreck my life forever.

I struggled to respond.

Look, I finally said, I wanna win too, but we're not going to war. If we lose, we lose.

His lip quivered before he protested.

But it is kinda like war! People die in war, and without basic income, we could have homeless people on the island, dying out in the cold like in America. And then no matter what I do in life, people will look at me and say, *That's the asshole who let in 20 goals against Italy and wrecked the island.*

He held a tissue up to his nose.

I'm just a kid, he said, muffled.

In that moment, ol' Barney's words swirled around me.

...you'll make your life's legacy over there in Greece ... be ready to step the fuck up.

Ok, I said, here's the plan. I'll play keeper tomorrow.

Stanley's face fell dumbfounded.

Have you even ever played keeper?

Of course. I'm cat-like. I played keep in a couple matches when we played the high school squads. I never let in a goal. I was like a cheetah.

I faced two, maybe three feeble shots on goal, but that information didn't seem relevant to share with Stanley at that juncture.

But, I said, here's the condition.

Stanley seemed eager to hear it.

You have to promise me that you won't quit. Because if you leave, here's what's gonna happen. We're gonna win the fucking gold medal, and you'll be watching me get carried off the pitch after I score the game-winning goal, the whole 80-thousand-person crowd clapping their asses off, and you'll say, *Goddamn me, I'm the Pete Best of Tiger Island.*

Stanley broke into a reluctant smile and threw his tissue in the basket. But then he said, sniffing, But if I stay, I did nothing.

That's not true. You made a save against England, didn't you?

One save. Whoopty do.

Yeah, but Italy was upset by England two days ago 1 - 0, and Costa Rica played out of their minds against them and only lost 2 - 1. So England's at the top of the table with six points, and we and Italy each have three points, but guess what?

What?

Because of *your* save, we're winning on goal differential. We have four goals for us and three against; Italy has two goals for and two against. So if we tie 'em tomorrow, we go through. If you wouldn't've come through for us with that save, we'd be facing a must-win. Now, it's a must-win or *tie*.

I pointed to my temple.

That's a big difference, psychologically, for the team's morale.

***

Coach Thomas made the announcement all business-like, like it wasn't insane for me to be in goal against the team who'd trounced us 10 - 0. I peeped at my teammates as she broke the news and witnessed something of a shockwave careen around the room. Their faces reminded me of how harebrained a scheme this really was.

Gregor, Joseph, and Eric warmed me up on the pitch. The stadium seemed nearly empty when we started, but within 45 minutes, spectators poured through the gates, over 31,000 of them, filling the place to capacity. Half the fans in the crowd wore our Tiger Island team shirts or Gregor's jersey from PSG.

With twenty minutes before kickoff, Gregor and Joseph sprinted up and down the sidelines with the rest of the team and played 3-on-2 keep away. Eric stayed behind and kept taking shots on me. He set four balls a couple feet apart from twenty yards out and blasted them.

His first shot, like a laser, flew not even a foot over the bar. I spit on Stanley's gloves and clapped them together. Eric stepped to the next ball and smoked it, and it came a few centimeters lower, striking the crossbar and shaking the frame of the goal. He hit the post again with his third shot, and before his fourth, he wiped his mop of curly hair out of his eyes, licked his index finger, and held it to the wind. Then he drained it on me. His shot had so much pace, and on top of that, he'd put some wicked English on it. It curled to the right like a sidewinding, heat-seeking missile; the shot left me frozen, watching the ball splash the net.

Set 'em up once more, I said. You can't do that again.

I'll get at least two more, he said. My sights are set now.

Eric scattered four balls five feet behind the 18, and he drained them all. Two of his shots bent and knocked off the side crossbar into the goal, one of which I dove for. Pure futility.

Why don't we have you taking free kicks?

I don't know. Gregor and Joseph seem to have it in hand.

Eric might have even surpassed his older brother Jules in skill by this point, but he hadn't shaken a minor case of little-brother timidity.

My arm fell around his shoulder while we made our way to the bench.

If we get a crack from inside 30, I said, I want you stepping up. Tell 'em up front, *this is mine motherfuckers*. And don't take no shit, ok?

Alright, Eric said with a laugh.

Tell 'em. Say, *I've had it with your shit*, and then say, *Fuck you, motherfuckers*.

163

I was pleased to get a grin out of him and loosen him up.

The defense gathered with me in a huddle before kickoff. I shouted above drums and chants from the packed stands.

The name of the game today is, *Get it out of here.* I suck at keeper, so pretend you have no keeper back here, ok?

I thought of Juwan Howard's refrain after Michigan's Fab Five reached the 1992 championship game.

Shock the world, I said, glove fist-bumping my defenders.

I ruffled David's blonde locks.

Go get 'em Davey.

Get off me, he said, shoving me away with a laugh.

I leapt and touched the bar of the goal a couple times. Gregor and Joseph jogged to center to start the match. My heart rampaged. The ref motioned back to me, and I held my glove up. He blew his whistle. The clock started ticking.

With not even a minute gone by, I was called into action. A grounder skipped to my right, and I smothered it. The next minute I snagged a threatening shot out of the air. Then I made an unorthodox kick save. And another diving one. The next one I punched over the goal for an Italian corner kick, then I plucked the kick out of the air. My saves verged on miraculous. My brain, spirit, and soul, all of it, stepped on to a different plane of existence, I think. I remember it now as a dream.

Seconds before half-time, with a clean sheet going, Andrea Pirlo, who'd ripped us for three of the 10 goals in 2000, threaded a beauty to his striker, Giuseppe Sculli. Sculli charged towards me with the ball stuck to his foot, ready to juke me one-on-one, but I slid towards him, hands up, trying to make myself as big as possible. His shot ricocheted off my right hand. Pirlo would've been there with the follow, but Jupiter, a step ahead of him, blasted the ball out of play. The ref blew for half-time.

Pirlo pointed a finger at me and leveled a strange accusation.

It's your birthday, isn't it?

The look on his face gave me reason to believe he might try to kick my ass. And *succeed*.

That's the only explanation for your lucky shit!

I shrugged and undid the Velcro of my gloves.

Restrained by a couple of his teammates, he said, Birthday boy, as if he was hurling a slur.

The Australian ref herded the two teams, deadlocked at 0 - 0, towards their respective dressing room tunnels.

My memory of half-time, too, remains foggy. I shook off any and all praise, like a baseball pitcher in the midst of a no-hitter. My teammates could tell. Anything that might cause me to think

165

of knockout-stage brackets, gold medals, sex, the finitude of life, my mother dead on the beach, spontaneous brain aneurysms, heart attacks, or anything else, I shushed. My transcendental state glided on the rails, unperturbed.

With some tactical adjustments courtesy of Coach Thomas, my defense proved more effective in the second half. Timothée and David forced the Italian offense to the outside, and the few crosses they sneaked through were gobbled up in the middle by Jupiter and Paul, or by Jules and Eric in center midfield coming back to help. On the other end, our offense was stymied as well. The most glorious stalemate of our lives appeared to be on the horizon.

But the lesson of England hung on my shoulders.

Joseph hit a shot towards their goal, which skipped too far left and rolled out for a goal kick. That's when I gathered my defense.

You think we're close? Anybody? Because let me tell you, we're *miles* away. We're Little Mac, and we're facing Mike Tyson right now.

Jupiter, who'd experienced a boyhood without Nintendo, scratched his chin, slightly flummoxed.

One punch, I said, and Tyson takes you out. They're mounting a final charge. Be ready, comrades.

Sure enough, Italy saddled up and grasped their inner overdogness. I dove outstretched and got my hand on a full-volley scorcher before David shuttled the ball away to safety. My next save, I later learned, tied me for the record in modern men's Olympic soccer. I got enough of a finger on the ball to redirect it into the post and then catch it bouncing back at me; I yelled with the spirit of a triumphant gladiator. I reckon though I sounded more like a piglet who'd been branded with a red-hot soldering iron.

I bounced the ball and paced around the penalty area. Four minutes remained until stoppage time. The crowd chanted something, but I couldn't tell what. I didn't care. After I punted the ball just beyond half-field, Italy came away with it and advanced to my left. I drifted towards the side of the action. They were stringing together passes brilliantly. I quaked, nearly mesmerized. A moment later, Pirlo had it within range. His fellow midfielder had threated a bullet to him, and he trapped it with an angel's touch before cracking a shot. Pushed too far to one side, out of position, I leapt through the air. The ball skipped once on the grass, like all my dreams skipping by, and sent a ripple through the net. A shockwave tore through the stadium.

Maximum volume poured from the mouths of every soul in attendance, and I laid on the ground, crushed, immobile, my ears ringing. Pandemonium and celebrations broke out all around me, and I buried my face in the grass and dirt.

I'll just burrow back in the earth from whence I came, I thought.

Coach Thomas grasped scraps of eleven fragile egos from the sideline.

Give me three more chances! We have time!

I slowly rose to my feet to see Gregor charging at me, full speed. He screeched to a stop in front of me and grabbed a fistful of my shirt, pulling my face within a centimeter of his. He had red, crazy eyes. He screamed.

Boo hoo motherfucker! Get that fucking look off your face this goddamn second!

My eyes got big.

We've come too far, he said, so this is what's gonna happen. You're gonna take off those gloves, pass me the ball, and I *will* score a fucking goal.

He released his grip on my shirt with a shove and bolted up the pitch to half-field.

I assumed he was serious, so I took off the gloves and keeper jersey. The fire swirled in my heart now too. I extended them to Jupiter and Paul. They could tell. Paul looked at Jupiter and grabbed the gloves and jersey. He draped his hand over my shoulder and said, I got you.

I slapped his butt and ran to the sideline for my number 55 shirt. Coach Thomas called out to Lucas.

Stay at the wing! We're leaving three in back!

Stanley tossed me my shirt and said, Hurry.

In the half-field circle, Gregor restarted the match, touching the ball forward to me, and I passed it back to Lucas. We failed to advance for three minutes, and just before an Italian shot whizzed by Paul's left post for a goal kick, the 90-minute mark came and went. Jupiter set up the goal kick. We knew this would be our last chance.

Etienne won the ball in mid-field and swung it up to Joseph who dropped it all the way back to Timothée in the defense. Timothée to Lucas on the wing, Lucas back to Timothée, and Timothée found me ten yards shy of mid-field. I trapped the ball and cut it right, then back left, juking and stutter-stepping, slicing my way through three Italian players. When two of them collapsed on me, I gave the ball up to Gregor. We'd practiced the give-and-go several million times, since Coach Thomas found us rocking grunge flannel, youngsters fast as lightening. I faked back and sprinted goalward. Gregor knew.

He hit me in stride, ahead of their last defender because I'd timed my run perfectly. With ninety-one and a half minutes gone by, I soared, the ball two feet ahead of me, towards a one-on-one with the best goalkeeper on the planet. Gianluigi Buffon, one of Italy's three over-23 players, was a three-year veteran of Juventus. I glimpsed how the next three seconds of my life would unfold: drift right and then cut the ball back left, sharply, and pass it with my left foot towards

169

the left post, curling it right, past Buffon, into the goal-- nay, into the pages of history. But an Italian demon hounded me, a step behind, not willing to allow me the one-on-one.

He clipped my right foot from behind, at full speed, and I flew face-first, sliding into the penalty area. With the whistling fury of a berserk tea kettle, the Australian ref charged towards us. I turned around in time, still laid out on the grass, to see a mob of Italian players obstructing him and his red card from their defender.

The ref marked our free kick one yard outside the penalty area, just right of center, and I popped up, spurred by a plan. I gathered Gregor, Joseph, Jules, Eric, Lucas, and Etienne in a huddle. David, Paul, and Timothée milled around the outside with Jupiter.

Everyone in this stadium knows who's taking this shot, I said. It's Gregor's ball.

Of course, Lucas said, everyone else nodding.

That's why I think Eric should take it.

That silenced everyone. I turned to the sweaty 20-year-old.

Do you want it, Eric?

Like an ice-cold assassin, he said, Yes. I want the shot.

I don't know if you all know, I said, but Eric was draining lasers on me all during warm ups. Bending ones.

Gregor had a huge grass stain, part of the

earth in fact, running across the front of his shirt. He gave me a hard look, like he was trying to deduce a lie, then he turned to Etienne, who seemed hesitant to offer an opinion. Finally, Gregor squinted and nodded, gazing downward, having retreated into his thoughts.

Eric takes it then, he said. Everybody crash.

Our huddle broke, but Gregor grabbed Eric's arm and said some intense word to him before picking up the ball and placing it at the spot of the foul. I ran to the right side of the box and saw Gregor lining up the kick, with Eric a couple yards behind him. I furrowed my brow. Joseph squeezed in to the left side with David and Etienne. All our defense and even Paul, who'd tossed his keeper gloves in the goal, pushed up with the rest of the offense.

Come in diagonal! Coach Thomas shouted from the sideline, motioning with her arm.

The ref tweeted his whistle, and Gregor galloped, ready to strike. I froze in disbelief at this clear betrayal. Flashbulbs burst all over the stadium and captured Gregor leaping three feet over the ball: a plan within the plan. The Italian wall broke, with two men hopping right. A couple paces behind Gregor, Eric blasted the shot, and it snuck through the opening. Buffon had lunged right when his wall flinched, and he'd need everything to recover. He dove but the ball kept bending left. I lost sight of it. Then the rapture happened.

171

***

Our whole team piled into the press conference room of Karaiskaki Stadium whether they wanted us there or not. A few of my teammates stood because there weren't enough chairs; we all huddled three or four each to a microphone.

A British reporter said, Ok, this question is for everyone, and the whole room erupted in laughter.

The place overflowed with reporters, activists, economists, conspiracy theorists, poets, comedians, and some of our friends. The electricity, and eclectic mix of people asking questions, reminded me of Bob Dylan's 1965 San Francisco press conference. A young Greek woman from a high school newspaper asked us, How do you feel after having achieved what may in fact go down, not only as one of the biggest upsets in Olympic soccer, but as one of the biggest upsets in the history of the Olympic Games?

David jumped in, reaching past his younger brother to grab a microphone.

If it's any indication, he said, when I die, on my tombstone, I want it to say: *Tiger Island 1, Italy 1.*

We and most the people there cracked up. An American reporter from the back fought through and said, This question is for Henri. Henri, does your performance tonight mean you'll be moving to keeper?

Hell no, I said, to laughs. Tonight could never be duplicated in a million years, so I'm ending my tenure as keeper on a high note. And I want to give props to our keepers Ezra and Stanley who came through for us in our first two matches. Without them, we wouldn't be in the position we're in tonight, where a tie gets us through.

Gregor, floating a black IWW baseball cap on his head, leaned over to me.

Goddamn good call tonight, brother. You were the architect.

We hooked index fingers and snapped our thumbs together.

A Greek anarchist philosopher, Takis Fotopoulos, asked us how we justified our participation in the games. Etienne fielded it.

We're here to build social capital, for the most part. We hope it'll allow us to launch a syndicalist pro team on Tiger Island, to help our archipelago economically and spiritually.

He added a final thought, speaking a tad quicker.

And ultimately, we're gearing up to fight the corporatist stranglehold FIFA and the IOC have on the game.

The room burst into a flurry of questions. People shouted over each other. Coach Thomas looked at her watch.

I'm afraid our time's up, she said.

Gregor spoke into the microphone.

We're out of time, but one last thing I want to tell the world: stay tuned. We're not done yet.

***

My freshly shorn Mohawk punched through an aerial ball from Etienne for my first goal of the tournament, and after Carlos Tevez drilled a brilliant equalizer for Argentina, Gregor drove home a left-footer for us to stun the world again and extend our road to the Promised Land.

In the semi-final match, Germany, who'd not surrendered a goal the entire tournament, stopped us dead in our tracks.

In our pre-match huddle, Coach Thomas said, Either thread the ball through to Gregor or Joseph, or stay back. We need to stay conservative and patient. If we blink, they score, and with their defense, there's no telling if we'll be able to get it back.

After ninety minutes, our conservative play yielded a stalemate. Ezra turned in a Jedi-like performance, with nine saves, deflecting two into the post, stopping hearts. The German keeper, Timo Hildebrand, frustrated Gregor all night, stoning him in two one-on-ones and plucking every cross from the air.

At our other forward position, Joseph frustrated himself. He had yet to score in the Olympics, in 2000 and 2004, though he'd struck the post three times and had seen a dozen of his shots whiz by the wrong side of the goal. At the 50th-minute mark against Germany, he drew a penalty kick but sent the ball barreling right at the numbers on Hildebrand's light blue jersey. Routine save.

In the twilight of two overtime periods, I knew in my bones some tragedy lurked for us in a penalty shootout. Three minutes shy of a full 120, Gregor's shot deflected off a German defender, out of bounds, and the ref awarded us a corner kick. Eric set the ball while five of us jockeyed for position among seven German players. I hoped for another late game stunner from Eric's efforts, but Hildebrand punched away the danger. It came to Jules, who trapped the ball with his chest and brought it down to his feet. Three Germans collapsed on him, and he sneaked the softest of passes between two of them, into the box. Joseph, who'd been so unlucky, was there.

From a standing position, no running up to it, he popped a one-timer that set all 32,000+ people in the stadium alight. I'm convinced no keeper on the planet could've stopped it. Joseph looked like an angel after the goal, joyfully wagging his head and finger *no*, as if even he didn't believe what'd just happened. Gregor, Etienne, Jules, and I mobbed him to the ground and others piled on.

In my duties as captain, before the match restarted for the final minutes, I felt it necessary to run up to every one of my teammates.

It's not over, I said. Keep your head in it.

Coach Thomas knelt on the sideline, biting a fingernail, and the rest of our team and staff locked arms. The ball ping-ponged all over the pitch for 190 tense seconds. Germany sent a last gasp of desperation into our box as the clock trav-

ersed 120 minutes. Jupiter headed it away. Timothée came screaming out of the backfield with the
ball and passed it up to Gregor. The Germans
were off guard, having pushed up too far for a final scoring attempt.

I charged up the pitch, particles of earth
spraying behind me. Seemingly bottomless re-
serves of joy and hope propelled me forward.
Gregor was contained by two German defenders
five yards shy of their box, and his two full seconds of keep-away footwork allowed me to span
thirty yards. He laid the ball off to the left side of
the pitch.

I've watched the last five minutes of that
match, on French TF1 TV, more times than I care
to admit.

In the last 60 seconds, the camera captures
an aerial shot from the left side of the pitch. Greg-
or slows down in front of the two German
defenders. He nudges the ball twice, steps over it,
and fakes a kick before making a cutback pass to
his left. I zip into the frame, shaved head - Mohawk gone - sprinting onto the slow-roller just
outside the box. After a single touch, I torch the
German keeper with a bending ball in the upper
right corner. The announcer screams into the microphone, *There's another one! That's the one that puts
it away!*

The coverage cuts to a young, blonde
German girl, flags painted on her cheeks, on the
verge of tears. Then we see Gregor run to me and

jump on my back while I'm motioning to a swath of our supporters in the ecstatic throng.

This match is over, the announcer says. *I don't believe it!*

They cut to footage of Parc Rochelle Baré back on Tiger Island. Two thousand people, maybe more, showed up to watch the match on a huge projected screen. They dance and hoist bottles of Champagne even though it was early morning there. The frame returns to our celebration, and a shot of Coach Thomas high-fiving Lucas and our team manager Lil' Rocky, an eighteen-year-old math genius from the island.

The announcer maintains his hyped tone and says, *Tiger Island wins 2 - 0 in a stunning finish! Saturday, in the gold medal match, they face unbeaten Brazil!*

Henri Sauvé
From an Undisclosed Location
Saturday, November 12, 2011

CHAPTER ELEVEN: Cinderella at the Ball

Gregor, Joseph, and I ate lunch on the outskirts of Athens after being the earliest risers of the team, at 11:00AM, the day after our semi-final victory. The sun beat down its blessings, and we claimed a table outside a stone café covered in green foliage. An ancient fountain bubbled in the center of the tiny square encircled by commercial buildings.

We perused the menu, and for a lark I said, Can I safely say that ancient Greece was mainly water, rock, and ideas?

Joseph's cheeks dimpled. I confessed to cribbing the line from my favorite poet, David Berman.

A young woman sat on the edge of the fountain, her eyes closed, and for a split second, I mistook her for Karen O from the Yeah Yeah Yeahs. She looked different than Karen O in the face but reminded me of the singer with her short black hair and fire engine red lipstick. On the DL, I pointed her out to my two mates.

Hair blacker than a stack of black cats, Gregor said, jumping his eyebrows up and down.

She pulled out a cigarette and put on headphones.

Go talk to her, Joseph said. Tell her your

Berman line.

Are you crazy? I said, my stomach dropping.

My nerves had sabotaged plenty of romantic opportunities in Paris. It didn't always use to be that way, like with Tiarne in Australia. Something happened after my panic attacks began. When talking with a woman, if the conversation made any sort of awkward turn, I'd think about how I could be screwing myself out of a lifetime of love and companionship.

I put off Joseph and his cheeky suggestion with an excuse.

But she's got headphones on.

You'll never know if you don't try, Gregor said. And besides, you're never gonna see her again in your life.

Just say hi and ask her where she's from, Joseph said, his smile bordering on mischievous.

I breathed deep and without warning, I stood up and walked over towards her, nestling into a spot a couple feet away from her on the ledge of the fountain. When the time came to talk, I chucked the script in my head.

I put my two trembling fingers to my lips and said, Do you have a ciggy I could have?

She peeled off her headphones and looked at me. I cleared my throat and said, Cigarette?

Oh sure, she said.

While she dug in her bag, I said, You speak English.

I do.

Where are you from?

Scotland. Edinburgh.

I nodded, debating whether to say something about her accent or Sean Connery. I thought better of it while she sparked me up.

Can you believe Greece is water, rocks, and ideas? I said.

Her countenance puzzled, and I choked and coughed on my cig.

Are you alright?

Yeah, I said coughing. This is just-- must be a different brand.

After a few seconds of dead air, I sensed she might put her headphones back on, so I said, So what brings you to Athens?

I'm volunteering in a medical tent for the Red Cross.

Are you an open-heart surgeon?

She laughed and shook her head.

No, I'm 19.

Gregor and Joseph watched me with encouraging, wide eyes. I tried not look at them.

I'm studying at Uni to be a nurse, she said. I thought volunteering here might give me a leg up, and I've always wanted to see Greece.

Are you a sports fan?

My nerves diminished a little each time our eyes met. I felt an overwhelming desire to make her laugh.

Sport? I don't know, I don't really care, but

the political aspect of the games I find sort of...

Interesting?

I was gonna say repulsive, she said.

In a comic way, I acted as if my body had just received a jolt, and she suppressed a laugh.

What do you mean? I said. Like with those construction workers getting killed?

Thirteen immigrant workers perished, pushed against the clock to build our Olympic dream in Athens.

Yeah, she said, the whole lot of it. They bus in migrants and rush 'em, and then people get hurt. The public pays the lion's share, for the games to happen, and it's always a few fat blokes walking away with millions.

She stubbed out her cigarette on the side of the fountain.

Everything they built here, she said, it's all gonna be ruins ten years on, I reckon. Ruins and debt.

I nodded with a sly smile.

You don't like sports, but you know the score. Say, what's your name?

Charlotte.

Charlotte, I'm Henri.

We shook hands.

Do you like walking?

I reckon, Charlotte said.

Do you like ice cream?

Sometimes, if it's good quality.

Charlotte, I have a confession. A *real* top 40

confession.

Uh oh, she said.

That was the first cigarette I've ever smoked.

In your entire life?

I shrugged with a guilty look.

I was just hoping to talk to you.

Her cheeks rouged.

Well, she said, you're lucky because I'm about to quit.

We watched some flapping seagull make off with a French fry, and I thought of my home.

Speaking of luck, I said, are you by any chance free tomorrow afternoon?

Her eyes squinted, and she smiled with a kind of playful suspicion.

I might be, if it's not another ruse.

No ruse. Just walking and talking and really good, high quality ice cream. We can meet right here at this fountain.

She appeared to swirl the idea around in her mind.

You might be interested to know, I said, I'm part of a new movement that's gonna change the Olympics. All of sports, actually. And I mean that as grandiose and insane as it sounds.

I stood up, feeling confident.

Charlotte laughed and said, Ok, I think I can manage to be here at 2.

I put on my purple-lens plastic sunglasses.

Charlotte from Edinburgh, I look forward

to seeing you tomorrow.

***

Charlotte wanted to help people, as a nurse, and she loved animals. She told me on our afternoon stroll.

Sometimes during rainstorms, she said, I look out the window and cry, thinking about all those homeless cats and dogs getting rained on.

Damn, I said, my eyes following the narrow, stony street.

I know, she said. I just wish I could adopt them all.

Are you gonna be one of those cat ladies someday?

Hopefully, if I can. I've only got one now. A grey cat back home named Harry Potter. We call him Harry Pot Pot, or just Pot Pot for short.

Pot Pot, I said, a smile bouncing to my lips. You know, I used to meow and drink milk from a bowl when I was a youngster.

Why'd you stop?

I don't know. My dad hated it. Once when he told me to knock it off I hissed at him.

The juxtaposition of Charlotte's black, long-sleeve Ramones t-shirt against the medieval facades around us made me feel like I was at a non-linear time party. (We had one of those once on the island. I came as an American pilgrim wearing a Nintendo Power Glove.)

So, she said, tell me about your grand plan to revolutionize sport.

Sports and society.

She nodded, Right, sports and society.

Ok, I said. I'll try to go fast because I don't want to bore you.

I breathed deep before talking fast.

I'm involved with two major soccer-syndicalist movements. That's where the players, workers, and the community collectively manage a revenue-generating team. The first and most important one to me personally is on our island. Tiger Island. In Lake Michigan. That's where I'm from. Have you heard of us? Anyway, we're trying to launch an MLS expansion franchise - that's the US professional soccer league - the profits of which would sustain our basic income, which is the best policy on our island in my opinion.

I put my hands on my knees and acted like I was out of breath.

How's it working out?

Strong, I said in a deep voice. Good momentum. Solid. If we win gold, we're golden, meaning we get the MLS franchise and save our way of life.

I reckon I'll be checking the papers for Olympic football news now, Charlotte said, for the first time in my life.

She took my arm, and my heart rate ticked up a notch. The street was quiet. I should have just enjoyed the moment, but youthful enthusiasm is so very hard to contain.

And the second one, I said, holding up my

index finger. Elevator pitch: this group my friends and I are supporting in Athens is advocating worker and community control of the Olympics. And to make Greece the all-time hosts of the Summer Olympics from now on.

Charlotte's eyebrows leapt up.

I like it, she said, but--

She thought for a second.

--wouldn't it be better if the Olympics just disappeared?

In all honestly, the thought had never occurred to me.

Yeah, I said slowly. I'd say if they don't change, they'd be better off gone.

I don't know why I felt it was an opportune time, but my hand slowly found hers.

I like that you think about the politics of sport whereas most people just watch, she said.

We promenaded. Love Makes You Feel Ten Feet Tall by the Velvet Underground rambled in my head. Charlotte told me about her older sister and younger brother, and her mother and father.

What do your parents do? I said.

Well, my dad owns a chain of slaughterhouses.

Jesus, I said, blindsided.

Charlotte cracked up.

I remembered you're vegetarian, she said. I just wanted to see your face. Too good. Really, he drives a bread truck.

Oh. I'm just glad he's not hacking up Wilbur from *Charlotte's Web*.

No, he doesn't do that. But he is pretty gruff.

You ever seen him cry?

Once, actually.

What happened?

He was cleaning a hunting rifle in the kitchen, and he shot a hole in the floor. My mother was standing four feet away. She told him, *If that ever happens again, I won't think twice about leaving you.*

Whoa.

He sobbed, Charlotte said, and told my mother down on his knee, *I'm sorry, Jenny. I can't believe I's so careless. I swear to Christ it'll never happen again.*

Charlotte shrugged.

She forgave him.

And he's never cried or blasted a hole in the kitchen floor since, I said.

A gun's never crossed our home's doorway since that day, she said. Keeps 'em all in the barn.

We arrived back to the square where we'd met.

So, I said, my team is playing in the gold medal match on Saturday.

PSG?

Tiger Island, I said, with slight disbelief.

Charlotte furrowed her brow.

Tiger Island has a football team?

Yes, I said, comically indignant, channeling George Costanza. We're like rock stars! That's the one I was just telling you--

She flashed a wicked grin. We reveled in flirtatious teasing until her taxi rumbled to a stop on one of the adjacent side streets of the small Athenian square. I handed the driver a 20 euro note. Charlotte protested.

How about you get the next one, I said.

The next one, eh?

I kissed her on the cheek and inhaled her scent, the most pleasing I'd ever smelled, even with a tinge of cigarette. I whispered in her ear.

Tomorrow?

***

Charlotte and I had a picnic in the National Gardens the next day in between my five-hour morning practice and late afternoon team meeting with Greek syndicalists and activists. She showed up with a Walkman cassette player. After we noshed and chatted in the grass for a bit, I asked, Whatcha been listening to?

Daniel Johnston. You know 'im?

I shook my head no.

She held out her headphones, offering. I put them on, pressed play, and laid my head on her Scottish thigh. Johnston crooned True Love Will Find You in the End while she petted my buzzed black hair in the sun. The shirtsleeve of her other arm resting on my chest slid up a few centimeters, revealing a bunch of thin, vicious-

188

looking lacerations. The notion struck me that I'd never seen her in short sleeves. My eyes darted up to her face, serene as could be. Her gaze drifted a kilometer up ahead, towards some palm trees, and after a few seconds, she caught me looking at her. She smiled, and I smiled back. She kept petting me, and I closed my eyes.

You wanna be my date to our team dinner tomorrow? I said, peeling the headphones off my ears.

I sneaked an eye open a half-millimeter, to see her reaction. She fretted, her teeth pressed together.

No offense, she said, but would I be the only non-footballer?

I sat up, shielding the sun from my eyes with my forearm.

They'll be *tons* of non-footballers. My brother's wife, Renée. Joseph's girlfriend, Linda. Paul's boyfriend, Freddy. You can meet my sister and nephew too, if you wanna. Oh, and we're all pitching in for flowers and a big gift for my coach. Her partner Rosa is pregnant.

Charlotte mulled it for a second.

What do people wear to a football dinner?

All-white tailcoat tuxedos, I said. The whole team.

Really?

I cracked up.

Naw, track suits and jeans and stuff. You'll do great.

Charlotte scoffed and sprinkled a handful of grass on my head.

***

At the dinner, Lucas and Jules sneaked in a boom box and a couple CDs. The spacey waves of *Eccsame The Photon Band* by Lilys rolled through the cozy, dimly lit restaurant room we'd rented. Charlotte held a Mai Tai and mingled with Ruth, Renée, and Linda. Gregor talked with our former captain, Angel, who'd flown up from Equatorial Guinea to support us. Angel ended up dropping out of med school, but he landed on his feet with an administrative position where he always wanted to be, with *Médecins Sans Frontières*. Joseph and David played with Arthur, who chased after a mini soccer ball. In front of a table of full of flowers and gifts, Coach Thomas and Rosa, whose belly was already showing, told a story to Etienne, Paul, Freddy, and Georges, our former goalkeeper. He flew in all the way from Lincoln, Nebraska, where he lived as a member of a Sudanese art collective. Timothée and Jupiter conspired together about something, jubilation on their faces. The younger guys - Ezra, Eric, Roland, Stanley, and Lil' Rocky - looked sharp in thrift-store sport coats while they carried on together.

My gaze drifted from one side of the room to the other. It was like Gregor said that one time; it was all our generation. Charlotte found me, awed by the scene from a discreet back corner. She said, How're you doing?

I nuzzled her cheek and said, I have to kiss you.

She smiled, and we kissed. The first one. Kurt Heasley's shoe-gazey guitar bent and wobbled with the candles on each table. Charlotte embraced me, kissed me on the neck, and lay her head on my shoulder. The whole archipelago felt perched up there too, on my neck and back, pressing on me. The weight of the living and the dead, my past selves, and people I'd never met. I loved them dearly. Still do. Always will. Charlotte reared her head back and lifted her hand from my waist up to my chest.

Henri, are you ok? Your heart's pounding.

I brought my hand there. The room spun.

Oh shit, I said.

I felt my face flush red with panic.

I need to go to the hospital, I said. This is it this time. The big one.

Henri Sauvé
From an Undisclosed Location
Sunday, November 13, 2011

CHAPTER TWELVE: With the Chips All In

Cleats clopped on the concrete in the tunnel at Olympic Stadium in Athens. We marched single file, side-by-side the Brazilians, who sported their iconic yellow jerseys, blue shorts, and blue socks. I was one of thirteen of us who wore black t-shirts over our traditional Tiger Island kits. We meant to mourn and honor the thirteen migrant workers who'd perished building stadiums for the games, though we'd reveal the symbolism of our shirts after the match, when announcing our support for the Greek All-Time Olympic Movement.

Light forced its way through the mouth of the tunnel and vanquished the panic I'd felt. Instead, I had the sensation of soaring above the clouds, or being a cloud. The only other day I'd felt a feeling like that was the morning of Gregor and Renée's life-union. Maybe the morning of the stadium vote when we were kids.

We exited the tunnel two-by-two, and encircling us, 82,000 spectators cheered at full blast. Brazil sprinted onto the pitch once they reached the touch line. Our squad lined up on it shoulder to shoulder. Coach Thomas, in a tailored black suit with a black skinny tie, said she wanted to give her team talk on the pitch, not in the locker room.

Look around, she said stone-seriously,

shouting above the gathered mass.

All 15 of us surveyed the crowd, already at capacity. Dozens of kids had their faces painted like tigers, and a section of fifty middle-aged women wore black dresses with red half-dollar-sized fleur-de-lys all over them, a traditional-style dress on the archipelago since the 1910s. Plenty of Brazil fans populated the stands, and other people seemed just to hate us with a passion, with no allegiance to either side. Five people unfurled a bed sheet with the simple message, *We Hate Tiger Island*, painted on it in English.

Coach Thomas' stoic look broke, and she beamed.

Can you believe this? Can you believe we're here? They're watching in Martinique, and they're definitely tuned in back home on the island. All over the world.

Gregor and I exchanged a hyped glance, and Ezra draped his arm around me. We fist bumped.

All you today baby, I said softly to him out of the corner of my mouth. Coach Thomas continued.

I'd like you all to think about getting here. And I'm not just talking about a 12-hour flight. Think to our first organized match, the critics, the 6AM-to-noon practices, the weight room, losing 10 goals to zero, and avenging 10 zero: think of all of it. The sweat. An injury you've overcome. Think of any time you thought you might quit.

Think of your personal journey, everyone who's ever supported you, then think of what we've done as a team.

She let us meditate on that for a half minute. Visions of my mother rushed through me, of Gregor, Ruth, Arthur, and even my father, along with big wins and crushing defeats. Subzero mornings, training on the island. I thought of Charlotte too, and how knowledgeable and compassionate she seemed during my episode the night before.

Now think of the future, Coach Thomas said, of what's at stake. The fate of our archipelago hinges on you, a three-goal underdog. There's 185 million people in Brazil. We represent 93,000. They're the U-23 section of the most storied side in history of the game. *Pelé* is cheering them on. Who are you? How are you gonna respond?

Joseph yelled, *Allez les gars!*

My teammates and I jumped up and down, giddy. Jules and Jupiter peeled off their black t-shirts. My stomach did backflips inside. We formed a circle. Coach Thomas yelled above drums and chants from the crowd.

No matter what today, we play *together*! They have all the weapons to pick us apart, but we're not gonna let 'em. We've come too far.

The sun shone through a cloudless sky thirty minutes before midday. The scent of freshly shorn grass filled my nostrils. I breathed it in deep. My right arm felt cold. I was attuned to every ping and ding in my body. I spoke out loud to myself at one point.

Shut it off for 90 minutes, then you can go die. You *will* give me the next 90.

During our warm-up, to bury my anxiety, I played hypeman, high-fiving my teammates and barking praise.

Great save Ezra! There you go David. Jupiter. No one's getting past the Island Curtain today.

I chased the ball in 3-on-2 keep-away with Etienne, Timothée, Joseph, and Gregor when the ref called me to center field for the coin toss. I shook hands with Brazil's captain, Ronaldinho, one of three over-23 players on their side. He was the reigning FIFA Player of the Year and a World Cup champion. If I wasn't playing in the match, I'd have probably asked him to take a picture with me. He won the toss and elected to kick off the match.

We lined up for the Brazilian and Greek national anthems. Because we didn't have a national anthem, usually the stadium announcer wouldn't say anything after the other team's played, but before the final, he said in English, French, and Greek: *The Cooperative Commonwealth on the Tiger Islands has no national anthem but wishes to express solidarity and goodwill to all creatures of earth.*

It makes us sound like space aliens, Gregor said with a smirk.

We huddled. Coach Thomas met every pair of eyes in the huddle before she said, You know the lineup. You know the game plan. Win together.

She strolled back to the bench, staring off towards the crowd. I screamed at the top of my lungs, Win together on three!

1-2-3, win together.

We broke and jogged to our positions. Gregor caught up to me and threw an arm around my shoulder, his hand reaching up to my very short hair. He pulled my head towards him.

Today is ours, brother. We always knew.

With a big grin shining, I said, *Allons-y mon frère.*

The Greek referee blew his whistle, and Ronaldinho touched the ball forward to begin the match. From the jump, both sides gave the capacity crowd everything: brilliant passes, ferocious tackling, heart-stopping saves, and raw emotion. The only thing that remained on their wish list at halftime was goals.

Throughout the course of the match, I took mental snapshots of the contrast of our white jerseys with red numbers against their yellow ones. I knew I'd see the Tiger Island-Brazil color combination and think of this matchup for the rest of my life.

Our breakthrough came in the 67th minute.

Timothée put together a give-and-go with Jules, creating enough space for himself to run with the ball at his feet. When two Brazilian midfielders collapsed on him, Timothée sent a bending rope of a pass to Etienne on the left side of the pitch near mid-field. Etienne cut the ball around one Brazilian player, who recovered and made a questionable tackle from behind. The Greek official wasn't having it.

Eric, Gregor, Etienne, Joseph, Jules, and I circled up.

Gregor said, Eric, can you hit this?

It's too far, he said, but I could send it into the mix.

Etienne suggested passing the ball outside and attempting to cross it to center. Joseph lobbied for Eric to try a shot on goal nevertheless. A distinct pain shot through my head. Something neurological, I was sure. Maybe an aneurysm. The panicked dizziness grabbed me again, and I stepped out of the huddle. Gregor saw me.

Henri, what's wrong?

I think I need to be subbed out, I said with my hands on my head. Something is seriously happening to me.

My teammates accosted me with their bulged eyes. Only Ruth and Charlotte knew what had happened the night before. Gregor put his hand on my shoulder. My hands trembled, and I held them up in front of my face, as if they'd offer some clue.

Listen to me, Gregor said. Close your eyes. Do it.

I squeezed 'em shut, which turned 'em to

little dams, keeping tears as bay. Gregor's voice alone occupied my consciousness.

Hear the crowd, he said. Feel them. It's purring.

He grabbed both my shoulders and touched his forehead to mine.

Now, think of a song. Breath in as deep as you can and remember the lyrics.

I filled my lungs and exhaled and an old folk ballad struck up in my head, loud as life - one of Bob Dylan's bootlegs from the night we played cards, when Davey shined a light on the MLS plan to save the spirit of our habitat. Dylan's timeless crooning washed against me: *I will not go down under the ground / 'Cause somebody tells me that death's comin' 'round / An' I will not carry myself down to die / When I go to my grave my head will be high / Let me die in my footsteps / Before I go down under the ground*

With another deep breath, the panic-hurricane sputtered out on my shores.

I want the kick, I said, wiping away a tear before it escaped my eyelid.

Gregor met the suggestion with a solemn nod.

There you go brother, he said, smacking his hand softly on my cheek. Let's seal this shit.

The ref blew his whistle hurrying us along.

Henri's hitting it! Gregor yelled, motioning the others to join him in a sprint to the box.

I placed the ball at the spot. The ref counted off ten yards. Coach Thomas pushed all our chips to the middle of the table. She shouted from the sideline, her hands megaphoned over her mouth, Defense, push up and crash!

David stayed back, the only one. Paul, Jupiter, and Timothée raced goalward. Flashbulbs sparkled all over the capacity stadium, even in the afternoon sun.

The free-kick felt wonderful leaving my boot. I struck it sweetly, sweeping just enough underneath to lift it without stubbing my foot. The ball floated in the air to the right of where I wanted it, but it would curl left still. First, Etienne leapt, then Timothée, followed by Jules and four Brazilian defenders. But they all jumped too soon. Or not high enough. The ball sailed over all of them. Gregor flew behind the leaping pack and extended his right foot, blasting the ball skyward. His full volley clanged the top crossbar and ricocheted back to earth. I remember the moment from a perspective outside my body. I can see myself running with my arms open, and the expression on my face when I learned that it'd gone in: That's how I want anyone who's ever known me to remember me after I die.

Fireworks exploded above 80 plus thousand, most of whom rejoiced. Our jam pile dispersed to restart the match.

Joy and unity propelled us; we controlled the ball with a hive mind. We'd been a team our whole young lives. Frustration gripped the Brazilian side, and with ten minutes remaining, they fell to pieces. We gobbled up their wayward passes in the midfield and won almost every 50/50. Ronaldinho had two or three of our players collapsing on him every time he touched the ball.

We entered stoppage time clinging to the 1 - 0 advantage.

Ezra yelled from between our goal posts, Just clear it! Keep it on their end!

They kept pushing though, searching for the equalizer. Kaká, another Brazilian legend, created space for himself and rocketed a ball from 27 yards out. I nearly shat myself. Ezra dove and deflected it out of bounds for a corner kick, a match-saving play. On TV, the camera cut to Pelé, biting his thumbnail. This would be the last chance for Brazil.

Every player piled into our penalty box, even Júlio César, Brazil's goalkeeper, another one of their three over-23 players. Etienne elbowed his way past two yellow jerseys. Gregor marked his man despite someone pulling a fistful of his shirt. Joseph stood in front of Ronaldinho at the touchline, hoping to trouble his corner kick. I shadowed Dani Alves, who would go on to play for FC Barcelona, as he weaved in and out of the teeming mass of players, each one jockeying for a miracle. Ronaldinho struck a line drive into the packed penalty area, igniting a ferocious struggle.

George Orwell claimed the Olympics was war minus the shooting. Perhaps he overstated the case, but I admit, both sides let loose some savagery. Elbows flew. Legs hacked. Heads butted. Hands grabbed collars and throats. Clumsy blows rained from every direction. 20 young men packed in a square, each one void of thought, propelled by instinct. The ball sneaked past lunging necks and heads, into the mix.

In the fateful scrum, Timothée poked the ball to Kaká, who wound up but didn't have enough room. Jupiter and Etienne flew at him, deflecting his shot. David beat me and Dani Alves to the loose ball and blasted it past half field, behind every Brazilian on the pitch.

Among a sea of souls, before my relationship with brilliant, beautiful Charlotte had unfolded, before my precious nephew had grown up tall and kind, before popular foment had restructured football to serve the people, before water privatizers had invaded our habitat, before we'd slashed truck tires on the mainland and sabotaged extraction wells, before the confluence of private capital and deadly force had unleashed death on our heads, before I'd suffered an event of deep physical consequence - the loss of my left leg below the knee, before we'd exposed and weakened the nightmare of Moloch by efforts which compelled my clandestine relocation: from a stainless steel whistle, the holy trinity pierced my ears and a roar went up from the people.

The Olympic Men's Football Team of the Cooperative Commonwealth on the Tiger Islands

Games of the XXVIII Olympiad
2004 – Athens, Greece

Roster

No	Name	Position	Age
#1	Ezra Taga	GK	20
#2	Gregor Heinrich	F	22
#3	Jupiter Agoot	D	22
#4	Joseph Atem	F	22
#5	Paul Feingold	D	21
#7	David Lefebvre	D	23
#12	Jules Solomon	MF	22
#13	Etienne Lefebvre	MF	25
#17	Eric Solomon	MF	20
#21	Timothée Vars	D	23
#55	Henri Sauvé (C)	MF	21
-Reserves-			
#0	Lucas Dujardin	MF	22
#10	Roland Lefebvre	D/MF	19
#25	Benjamin Berman	D	20
#99	Stanley Roth	GK	17

Coach: Abeba Thomas-Dupont

Group Table
Group D

	Pld	W	L	T	GF	GA	GD	Pts
England	3	2	1	0	5	3	+2	6
Tiger Islands	3	1	1	1	5	4	+1	4
Italy	3	1	1	1	3	3	0	4
Costa Rica	3	1	2	0	3	6	-3	3

Group Stage
9 August 2004
Pampeloponnisiako Stadium, Patras
Attendance: 18,895
Referee: Carlos Batres (Guatemala)

20:30 Tiger Islands 3 – 1 Costa Rica
Saborío 52'

Heinrich 61'
Dujardin 71'
Vars 81'

Group Stage
14 August 2004
Pampeloponnisiako Stadium, Patras
Attendance: 18,895
Referee: Carlos Torres (Paraguay)

20:30 England 2 – 1 Tiger Islands
Heinrich 39'

Owen 82' (pen.)
Sinclair 88'

Group Stage

17 August 2004
Karaiskaki Stadium, Piraeus
Attendance: 31,340
Referee: Mark Shield (Australia)
20:30 Italy   1 – 1   Tiger Islands
       Pirlo 86'   E. Solomon 90 + 2'

Quarter-Final
21 August 2004
Karaiskaki Stadium, Piraeus
Attendance: 32,115
Referee: Pedro Proença (Portugal)
21:00 Tiger Islands   2 – 1   Argentina
       Sauvé   9'

                                  Tevez '34
       Heinrich 50'

Semi-Final
24 August 2004
Karaiskaki Stadium, Piraeus
Attendance: 32,115
Referee: Benito Archundia (Mexico)
18:00 Germany   0 – 2   Tiger Islands
                              Atem 117'
                              Sauvé 120'

Gold Medal Match
28 August 2004
Olympic Stadium, Athens
Attendance: 82,662
Referee: Kyros Vassaras (Greece)

12:00 Brazil   0 – 1   Tiger Islands
                                      Heinrich 67'

"Historical Timeline of The Cooperative Commonwealth on the Tiger Islands 1760 - 2011" appears here courtesy of Professor Claire Patterson's *De la COMMUNE au COMMONWEALTH: HISTOIRE du COMMONWEALTH COOPERATIF DES ILES du TIGRE* (University of Tiger Island Press: 1993, 2011)

The following historical timeline was translated from the original French into English by Professor Jean Claude Renault in December of 2011. Archipelago population figures by decade are underlined.

1760 – 0

1761 - Guillaume de Beaulieu (1726 – 1789) and his team claim an uninhabited island, latitude 45.6667, longitude -85.5333, as *Poisson Ile* [Fish Island] for France. They find evidence that native peoples had passed through the island, though no proof of habitation.

1763 – Poisson Ile remains the only part of New France (upper Great Lakes territory claimed by France) not ceded to the Spanish or British.

1770 – 7

1775 – De Beaulieu and his associate, Simon Baré (1741 – 1792), return to Paris, promoting life on Poisson Ile. 35 men and 21 women depart France with de Beaulieu and Baré.

1776 – An early winter leads to the deaths of 14 people during their voyage to the island. Three of de Beaulieu's five remaining team members perish while he is away; the total population after his return is 46. Rochelle Baré (née Brûlé) (1755 – 1796), a former Parisian prostitute, then wife of Simon Baré, gives birth to the first child born on the island, a girl, Odette (1776 – 1824).

<u>1780 - 47</u>

1788 – After 12 years, with roughly 50 inhabitants homesteading faithfully through harsh winters, 22 inhabitants leave, citing the isolation and difficult conditions. De Beaulieu and Simon Baré depart on their second and final recruiting mission to the métropole.

1789 – De Beaulieu and Baré return in November with 158 new arrivals. The two men promise the new inhabitants a land of tranquility and plenty, far from the political and social turmoil of the *métropole*. Two thirds of the new arrivals are women, many of whom, like Rochelle Baré, have escaped life in the brothel.

One week after his return to Poisson Ile, de Beaulieu becomes intoxicated during a thunderstorm and gives what later comes to be known among anarchists and anti-authoritarians of all stripes as "The November Speech:" an impassioned yet articulate speech filled with revolutionary fervor, railing against alleged government corruption and wrongdoing and the related financial crisis in France.

In the culmination of the speech, de Beaulieu reportedly removes the French flag from his quarters, and wading into freezing Lake Michigan, declares to onlookers standing on the shore: "With Simon and the good working people, I have burned the fortress [the Bastille]. Every beast, child, woman, and man must revolt against tyrants, be they kings, rich merchants, or the Devil's Holy men. Revolt good working people or they will destroy your souls and all that is good on earth!"

De Beaulieu shouts these words before hurling the tricolor flag into the water. Moments later, lightning strikes the biggest pine tree on the island. De Beaulieu collapses in the shallow water of the lake and dies. The remaining inhabitants toil for their survival in relative isolation for the next 35 years.

1790 – 190
1800 – 245
1810 – 268
1820 – 340

1824 – Scores become stricken by a mysterious illness; dozens parish. Natural historians speculate the illness was likely the result of eating a diseased animal or poisonous plant. In an effort to find a doctor willing to come to the island, search parties dispatched to the upper and lower peninsulas of the Territory of Michigan exaggerate the scale of the illness. Still, no doctors arrive.

1830 - 290

1836 – Charles LaChance (1799 – 1851), a military commander charged with maintenance of the island, proposes that the name *Poison Ile* be changed to *Tigre Ile*, in an effort to intimidate Michiganders, whom he suspects will attack after they have achieved statehood. He orders a dozen agents to shoreline areas of the upper and lower peninsulas of Michigan to spread disinformation about mysterious illnesses and tiger attacks on the island. LaChance's mainland spies report that, in the matter of tiger attacks, they are disbelieved and ridiculed by those whom they encounter, mostly native peoples and Jesuit monks. The attack from Michigan never comes; LaChance is baffled.

1839 – LaChance, weary of life on the island, obtains permission to sell Tiger Island to the United States. Representing the U.S., Governor Stevens T. Mason (1811 – 1843) of Michigan refuses a meeting with LaChance, instead sending a written message by horseback to a French representative waiting in what is now Suttons Bay, Michigan. The message declares that the State of Michigan will not buy the island "for any price" due to the widespread belief among Michiganders that it and its inhabitants had been contaminated with a strange and deadly disease. Steady immigration from the French *métropole* bolsters the inhabitants' quiet efforts at subsistence for the next 32 years.

1840 – 310
1850 – 392
1860 – 527
1870 – 943

1871 – In the aftermath of the Paris Commune and the *"semaine sanglante"* ("bloody week") massacre, roughly 6,000 French women and men, mostly Parisian communards of anarchist character, arrive on Tiger Island. They flee to the island for its distance from Paris – many had been charged with serious crimes against the French state for their involvement in the commune insurrection – and because it had long remained in the radical imaginary in France due to the legacy of de Beaulieu and "The November Speech."

Following a fist-fight with the anarchist painter Georges Pontier (1840 – 1905), the appointed steward of the island, Colonel Jean Louis (1832 – 1901), returns to Paris with two hundred original inhabitants. The ex-communards begin talks with the originals, and among themselves, about remaking the island along democratic, egalitarian lines. They occupy the three large surrounding islands - Little Pea Island to the west, Wind Island to the north, and Butter Island to the north east - the major inhabited islands which today constitute the Tiger Island archipelago.

1872 – Unprepared for the harsh winter, 289 new inhabitants perish in January and February. By April, the inhabitants organize and collectively delegate necessary tasks through unions with rotating spokespeople. Other social affinity groups are represented in the monthly General Assembly (GA); 24 young women and five men establish the *Union des Femmes et Mères* (UFM – Union of Women and Mothers) in March. After months of collective deliberation, Tiger Island quietly secedes

211

from French control. Officials in Paris, who had hoped for years to sell the island, take no action. The archipelago graveyard on Wind Island is established.

1873 – Félix Giroux (1838 – 1912), spokesperson of the newly formed Diplomatic Council, meets with representatives of Michigan. Giroux and Governor John J. Bagley (1832 – 1881) of Michigan sign *The Tiger Island-Michigan Peace Treaty of 1873*.

1877 – After obtaining a printing press from anarchist activists in Chicago, ex-communards begin printing the archipelago's first weekly newspaper (which still exists as of this writing). *La Gazette Populaire* (*La GP*) contains daily news and essays from anarchist and anti-authoritarian perspectives.

1880 – 6,518

1881 – Amid brutal social conditions for Black Americans in the south following the end of reconstruction in 1877, 352 émigrés, mostly former slaves from New Orleans, Louisiana, seek habitation on the archipelago. They make the journey north after reading translated anti-Jim Crow articles originally published in *La GP*. Their arrival on the formerly racially homogenous islands prompts the passage of *La Première Resolution*, the first domestic legislative resolution recorded on the Tiger Islands.

La Première Resolution states: "No laborer or inhabitant of this archipelago shall heretofore be denied access to any role in the industrial or social spheres of life based upon judgment which considers the race of that individual."

1882 – In collaboration with 50 ex-communards and their children, two dozen Black Americans and their children form a language school in which lessons and conversation practice in English and French are exchanged.

1886 – 204 political and labor activists of anarchist character from the Chicago area immigrate to Tiger Island in the aftermath of the Haymarket Affair. Many flee following threats of arrest and other forms of police repression. Three hundred more Black Americans emigrate from Louisiana. Their arrival, along with the Chicago activists, solidifies the burgeoning bilingual pedagogy and practice, of French and English, on the archipelago.

1890 – 7,276

1894 – Following the passage of *Les Lois Scelerates* ("The Scoundrelly Laws") in France, virtually all anarchist publications in Paris are shut down and about a dozen writers and publishers go into exile on Tiger Island. Several, including Emile Pouget (1860 – 1931), begin writing for *La GP*.

1895 – After the two-year reign of dynamite, dagger, and gunshot (1892 – 1894); the "Trial of Thirty" (August-October 1894); and subsequent instances of police repression and public backlash, the anarchist community in Paris and much of France lies in ruins. 500 to 700 anarchist writers, theorists, and laborers of radical persuasion, immigrate to Tiger Island.

1896 - In their search for building materials, for homes and other structures, the inhabitants acquire and use money, U.S. dollars, for the first time on the island. Recent immigrants from France and the U.S. pool their meager resources into one *Bourse Collective* (collective purse), and they also accrue money from chopping down and bundling the seemingly plentiful pine trees which populate the island forest. They sell many bundles as cordwood to daily passing steamers. The builder's union erects more log homes and three large Finnish-style communal saunas.

1897 – The GA establishes the *Union des Espaces Publiques* (UEP - Parks and Coastline Union).

1898 – Inhabitants formally establish two primary schools, a high school, and the university, along with the island's first book bindery. The high school is named in honor of Ida Jasper (1834 – 1897), a former slave from Georgia who played a significant role in establishing the first language exchange between Black Americans and ex-communards in 1882. The progressive, democratic curriculum allows students to interact with one another across age-lines and follow their own interests in many domains. Abraham Robinson (1866 – 1939), a political theorist and son of former slaves, becomes the first professor at the University of Tiger Island (UIT).

1899 – La Galerie de l'Ile, the first art museum and gallery on Tiger Island, opens. Camille Pissarro (1830 – 1903), José Guadalupe Posada (1852 –

214

1913), and a young, unknown Francis Picabia (1879 – 1953) are among the opening night attendees.

1899 – Inspired by a lecture on sewing collectives by Rosa Luxembourg, 21 inhabitants, women and men, in conjunction with several artists who become the island's first clothing designers, establish *La Cooperative de Couture des Iles du Tigre* (The Sewing Cooperative on the Tiger Islands).

1900 – 8,471

1901 – U.S. Officials charge that ideas emanating from or associated with the anarchist press on the island had influenced Leon Czolgosz (1873 – 1901), assassin of President William McKinley (1843 – 1901). Czolgosz, a native of Alpena, Michigan, allegedly once visited Tiger Island and also claimed to have been influenced by anarchist writers there. The U.S. Congress dissolves *The Tiger Island-Michigan Peace Treaty of 1873* and enacts penalties - $1,000 fine and up to 5 years in prison – for any U.S. citizen who visits the islands. They also mount a two-year blockade against persons and goods coming from and going to the island. This begins the "70 Years of Enmity" between Tiger Island and the U.S. The commonwealth moves from using U.S. dollars (USD) to Canadian dollars (CAD), which remain the de facto currency of the islands as of this writing.

1903 – After anarchist threats and courthouse occupations by radical elements in New York, Chicago, and Detroit, the U.S. ends its blockade of the archipelago, but continues its commercial embargo until 1971.

1907 – After Lucy Parsons' (1853 – 1942) surprise visit, laborers on the islands form a General Membership Branch of the Industrial Workers of the World and join en masse. Necessary tasks had formerly been collectivized; however, the IWW provides laborers a framework with which to organize as one big union across all labor sectors. Elsa Lacriox (1880 – 1955), a member of the homebuilders union and later member of the Diplomatic Council, is quoted in *La GP*, "We join the IWW for the future. Our situation is much simpler here on the island [compared to Chicago] because, thank heaven, we are not creatures of the factory. We are creatures of the workshop, the garden, and the small farm."

1909 – A near unanimous vote in the GA disallows cars on the islands.

1910 – 9,479

1914 – The archipelago issues a collective statement condemning all participation in the war in Europe, which *The New York Times* and *Chicago Tribune* refuse to print. The statement does however appear in smaller circulation radical newspapers in Milwaukee and Chicago.

1919 – In an archipelago-wide vote drafted by the GA, inhabitants approve *The Declaration of Self-Determination and Free-Movement*. The GA formalizes the official diplomatic name of the archipelago: *Le Commonwealth Cooperatif des Iles du Tigre*, taken up in English as, The Cooperative

Commonwealth on the Tiger Islands. They issue "Commonwealth Cards" (*Les Cartes du Common-wealth*) to inhabitants residing on the archipelago at least three years' time, approved as permanent residents by their respective neighborhood associations. Commonwealth Cards are intended to help inhabitants move freely across borders, with rights, codified and guaranteed by a common-wealth of persons, recognized among the nations. 305 leave the islands voluntarily after the passage of *The Declaration of Self-Determination*, citing the demise of the post-commune, anti-statist, libertarian project.

1920 – 11,114

1922 – First use of neighborhood "Kangaroo Courts." Punishments range from washing dishes to the rare expulsion from the archipelago.

1930 – 15,367

1930 – Over 6,000 American workers take up residence on Tiger Island. They are greeted with IWW tracts which promise to all laborers and their families "an escape from the skullduggery of politics and the capitalist class. On Tiger Island, workers are accorded the full fruits of their labor!"

Management of the *Bourse Collective* is taken up by the newly formed *Association des Affaires Sociales de l'Archipel* (AASA – Association of Archipelago Social Affairs), whose members are recallable and selected through a volunteer lottery. AASA resolutions require approval by the GA or by an archipelago-wide majority vote.

1932 – Amid disturbing antisemitic social developments in Europe, roughly 8,000 European Jews arrive in what some inhabitants referred to colloquially as the first "Anarchist Aliyah." A majority of the new émigrés are from France, while several thousand are from Germany and Poland. Some three hundred have come from as far as Moldova and the Ukraine.

1933 – Laborers work through cold temperatures to complete the *Centre des Besoins Sociaux* (CBS – Center for Social Needs) by November. The CBS is located on the upper east side of Tiger Island, just south of the harbor. The center, funded by the *Bourse Collective*, includes emergency medical services, doctors' offices, and fire and rescue services. From its opening to the present era, the CBS provides all services free-at-the-point-of-delivery; abortions for females of any age, at any stage in pregnancy, are available on demand, with no questions asked.

1936 – In April, 68 inhabitants travel to Zaragoza, Spain to witness and write about the CNT (Spanish National Confederation of Labor) national congress in May. All 68 remain in Spain and join the International Brigades. 17 are killed in combat against the fascists. After the end of the war, 10 move to France, and 41 return to Tiger Island. Those returning arrive with 45 Spanish nationals, a dozen of whom later found the free sex commune on Little Pea Island.

1937 – With a population which has swelled above

30,000, and with dozens of Jewish refugees arriving weekly, the 947 inhabitants in the IWW builders' union begin a massive housing construction project. They build many of the Swiss chalet-style homes which define the architectural character of the residential district in the current era. With the new construction, indoor plumbing and electricity through hydroelectric power generation steadily becomes available on the islands. Electricity for the island grid is also generated by water-wheels and stationary bikes. Laborers and scientists from the University of Tiger Island establish the wastewater treatment facility on the southwestern tip of Tiger Island. Homes are deeded by need to the elderly, families with infants and children, and individuals with special needs, then by location to CBS workers, members of the IWW builder's union, and finally, by lottery to the general population.

Amid the residential expansion, inhabitants approve a measure to preserve space for a park northwest of the agricultural fields. Upon a proposal from the UFM, the park is named *Parc Rochelle Baré*, in honor of the first woman to become a mother on the island.

1938 - The archipelago reaches a deal with the Canadian government for disposal of its Municipal Solid Waste. Telephone lines are installed throughout the archipelago.

1940 – 37,656

1940 – The Armistice Day Blizzard blankets the is-

219

lands in over two feet of snow, which is accompanied by 100 kilometer per hour winds. Six perish as a result of the rapid temperature drop and extreme winds.

1942 – A group of 76 men and 24 women, henceforth known as "The Honorable 100," secure arms from syndicalist allies in Canada en route to the *métropole* to join *La Résistance Française*. 86 reportedly die in live sabotage missions against the Nazis. The remaining 14 spend the rest of their lives in exile in various parts of Europe. At least six more squads, averaging around 12 inhabitants each, leave Tiger Island to join *La Résistance* throughout the war years.

1943 – On June 4, a small cabin cruiser washes ashore on the western beach of Little Pea Island. Inside the boat, one of the members of the free sex commune discovers Kermit Roosevelt (1889 – 1943), son of U.S. President Theodore Roosevelt, dead of an apparent self-inflicted gun-shot wound. The Roosevelt family, not wanting to upset the fragile health of Kermit's mother, Edith, reports the cause of death as a heart attack and pursues no charges against the archipelago.

1945 – The Avi Solomon School of Law at the University of Tiger Island is founded with a generous donation from three separate families, Jewish refugee émigrés, in honor of their friend, Avi Solomon (1901 – 1943), who was sent from Drancy to Bergen-Belson where he was killed.

1946 – In August, the UEP erects a monument in

the northwest corner of Parc Rochelle Baré to "The Honorable 100" and all others who left to join *La Résistance.*

1948 – Beginning on May 15, continuing through the end of the month, *La GP* and *The Chicago Tribune*, among other publications, are flooded with letters from (mostly Jewish) inhabitants of Tiger Island. They lament the establishment of the State of Israel and express their opposition to the creation of the state. Throughout the 1930s and 1940s, they had supported the creation of a singular, secular state in Mandatory Palestine, one which favors no religion or ethnicity and which promotes equal rights, Arab-Jewish cooperation, as well as collectivized, unionized labor in the Wobblie-shop model.

1949 – In March, in an archipelago-wide vote drafted by the GA, proposed by the UEP, inhabitants approve the designation of Wind Island as the site of a nondenominational, spiritual ashram. Following the passage of the resolution, the island attracts many Native American visitors who perform spiritual ceremonies prohibited in the U.S. (Native Peoples do not achieve spiritual freedom in the U.S. until 1978, with the passage of the *Native Indian Religious Freedom Act.*)

1950 – 55,172

1952 – *Harper's Magazine* publishes an article, "The Red and Black Island, Now Vegetarian," after, out of popular agitation and agricultural necessity, meat consumption on the archipelago plummets

221

by 80% over a five-year period, concurrent with the massive proliferation of yard gardens.

1953 – After two years of work, the IWW builders' union completes construction of 992 visitors' homes. The homes wrap along the outer edge of the residential district, towards the western shore of Tiger Island. They are expected to generate revenue for necessary community institutions such as the CBS, the UEP, the AASA, and the University of Tiger Island, among others. Housekeeping and maintenance duties of the visitors' homes are shared collectively by all adult permanent residents of the archipelago. On average, each adult devotes 24 hours of labor annually towards visitor housing duties.

1955 – Collective revenue surges on the archipelago over the next five years. The main sources of revenue include tourism/visitor housing, industrial dues, domestic marijuana sales, as well as export sales of beer and root vegetables (sugar beets and potatoes) to Canada from the *Jardin Collectif* (Collective Garden).

1956 – The AASA, vested by an archipelago-wide vote, establishes basic income, at 200 Canadian dollars annually, paid monthly to Archipelago Card-holders 19 and older. Working hours begin to gradually decrease over the next 30 years.

1958 – Dr. Jonas Salk (1914 - 1995) serves as keynote speaker at the opening ceremony of the University of Tiger Island Medical School. Dr. Salk's appearance sways U.S. public opinion in fa-

vor of ending the embargo against the archipelago, though it remains in place for another 13 years.
1960 – 64,283
1961 – First Annual Tiger Island Jazz Festival takes place at the end of May.
1962 – Through an archipelago-wide vote drafted by the GA, the inhabitants approve construction of a small airport on Butter Island. Various aircraft, ranging in passenger capacities of 25 to 120, fly non-stop to and from Toronto. Flight schedules range from two or three arrivals and departures per day from mid-April to mid-September, to three flights per week during the winter months.
1965 – Documents leaked by CIA whistleblower James Clark (1918 – 1991) reveal that CIA agents monitored activities on Tiger Island throughout the 1950s and stole preliminary blueprints of the airport on Butter Island before it was built. The documents also reveal that several of President Dwight Eisenhower's advisors urged him to approve CIA sabotage operations against the archipelago, though he did not grant their approval. As a result of the disclosures, the AASA proposes all incoming vessels and persons register at the northeast harbor before entering Tiger Island. They also propose six "lighthouse lookouts" be erected along the perimeter of the island to ensure all vessels and persons enter through the harbor. These proposals are rejected by the GA on the basis that they would lead to the creation of a militarized border apparatus but would not suc-

ceed in stopping CIA infiltration.

1966 – *La Première Resolution* is updated to include gender, age, sexual orientation, and personal spiritual choice.

1967 – Noam Chomsky (b. 1928) visits the archipelago in late July to deliver a lecture on language acquisition and generative grammar at the University of Tiger Island's School of Languages and Literature. He also presents a lecture outdoors, at Parc Rochelle Baré, on the Vietnam War and war resistance, in addition to participating in a roundtable discussion on industrial unionism with elected officers of the Tiger Island IWW General Membership Branch.

1969 – Island sociologists estimate that approximately 200 young men avoiding the U.S. military draft moved to the island between 1969 and 1971.

1970 – 71,684

1971 – In February, the U.S. President Richard Nixon lifts the embargo, formally ending the "70 years of enmity," though a great deal of ideological enmity remains into the modern era between the archipelago and the state-corporate power elite of the U.S. The decision to lift the embargo comes after a great deal of pressure within the U.S. from activist elements, but also from the U.S. business community.

Noam Chomsky has pointed out that the U.S. did not move to normalize relations with the archipelago even though a majority of its citizens supported such a move for more than a decade.

He claims that business pressure, for example Alonzo G. Decker, Jr. (1908 - 1989), CEO of Black & Decker, writing an open letter to President Nixon in favor of normalization, prompts the change in U.S. policy. According to Chomsky, on the subject of the archipelago embargo, "The situation with Tiger Island [...] is another one of those instances where U.S. officials have suppressed democracy for decades but scrupulously attended to the interests of big business. It's another example that illustrates how the U.S. is a business-run society to an unusual extent in the developed world."

Approximately 3,000 Americans emigrate to Tiger Island within two months of the embargo's end; this wave of migration is known colloquially as the first "artist Aliyah," because of the high number of artists, filmmakers, and writers among the émigrés.

The archipelago moves to biweekly solid municipal waste disposal, picked up by Hiawatha Shores, a company in the upper peninsula of Michigan, which saves twelve million Canadian dollars annually in solid municipal waste disposal costs.

1972 – The First Annual Tiger Island Film Festival takes place at the end of July. Ellen Burstyn and Jack Nicolson, promoting *The King of Marvin Gardens*, are among some of the notable actors who attend the festival. Director Alfred Hitchcock also attends the festival and is interviewed in front of a capacity crowd at the *Cinema de la Cité* following a screening of *Frenzy*. Elana Gold (b. 1930), the foremost film scholar at the University of Tiger Island, conducts the interview, which is later broadcast on BBC Radio.

1973 – The IWW Builder's Union demolishes the island's original indoor activity center and builds its contemporary incarnation.

1974 – A white supremacist, Lee Kennedy (1925 – 1992), opens fire from his small fishing boat, killing two people on Tiger Island's western beach. He is apprehended later that day by the Michigan Coastguard and is held in custody by the State of Michigan for three months while The Commonwealth approves the building of a small detention center on Butter Island*; one did not exist on the archipelago previously. Kennedy receives a trial by jury on Butter Island in November and is sentenced to 21 years preventive detention.

*In the detention center, detainees receive counseling, supervised interaction with animals, and access to supplies for artistic or written projects. The rates of incidents punishable with preventive detention on the archipelago are the lowest in developed countries. As of 1993, there are 14 detainees in the 160-room detention center, out of a permanent population on the islands of over 90,000. The recidivism rate for men is 5% since the founding of the detention center, and of the nine women who have been held in detention, none have reoffended.

1975 – The GA drafts a contentious archipelago-wide vote, approved by a slim margin, which establishes *Les Forces de Defense de Peuple des Îles du Tigre* (*Les FD* – Defense Forces of the People on the Tiger Islands). Les FD are headquartered in the CBS and are permitted to carry small firearms, one Commonwealth-issued 7.65mm that they must surrender when off duty. Les FD are not permitted to issue tickets or to "police the archipelago." Their authority is limited to two types of situations: those in which one's life may be under threat due to violence, or those situations in which individuals from outside the islands arrive to threaten the lives of inhabitants. The patrol jurisdiction of Les FD is limited to island perimeters, from water to 20 meters inland, by boat or on foot; they are not permitted to patrol anywhere else on the archipelago. At the time of their establishment, the Turonensis neighborhood association issues a declaration indicating that if they see uniformed FD in the residential district for reasons other than those specified in the FD charter, they intend to unite in a posse to disarm all FD and burn their quarters in the CBS. Les FD begin armed, coastal patrols in February.

1977 – In September, Delphine Gauthier (b. 1950), Anna Jones (b. 1953), and Violet Winslow (b. 1949), all Archipelago Card-holders and members of the UFM, are arrested in Vevey, Switzerland. They are charged with property destruction via arson totaling 90,000 Swiss Francs in an incident which took place at Vevey Corp corporate headquarters. The women maintain that their actions were in response to the unnecessary suffering and deaths of babies in developing nations which they claim have been caused by Nestlé's disingenuous and aggressive marketing of breast-milk substitutes. Gauthier and Winslow are sentenced to ten years in prison in Switzerland; Jones eight. Switzerland additionally requests extradition of two other Archipelago Card-holders whom they claim evidence suggests were involved in the incident; Miriam Sloman (b. 1931), spokesperson of the Diplomatic Council, issues a statement refusing to comply with the extradition request and further demands that the three women in custody be deported to the archipelago. The Swiss refuse. These events, known on the archipelago as *The Vevey Corp Affair of 1977*, garner widespread media attention and contribute to a growing boycott in the U.S. against Vevey Corp for its allegedly unethical marketing practices of infant formula.

1980 – 83,929

1980 – Steady immigration from France, Canada, the U.S., and various parts of Europe continues throughout the 1980s.

1981 – In solidarity with activists in San Francisco, the archipelago holds, in late June, an "International Lesbian and Gay Freedom Day Parade." In the years following, up to the present, "The Lesbian and Gay Freedom Festival on Tiger Island" takes place during the last weekend in June.

1982 – The first computers arrive on the archipelago. The University of Tiger Island purchases 65 TRS-80 computers from the Tandy Corporation. The students learn basic computer language, basic functions, and communication interfaces.

1986 – A study released by Central Michigan University concludes that the archipelago produces 80% less municipal solid waste than U.S. cities of comparable population. Researchers attribute the relatively low amount of solid waste to the absence of processed or packaged foods, the relatively low rate of purchases of material consumer goods, and the durability of material consumer goods produced on the islands.

1988 - *La Première Resolution* is updated to include physical ability and appearance.

1989 - 65 émigrés, eight adults with 57 orphaned children, all from the Sudan, arrive on the archipelago in April.

1990 – 91,127

1993 – Philippe Benjamin (b. 1951), spokesperson of the Diplomatic Council, is shut out of all talks pertaining to NAFTA and his remarks sent to major U.S. newspapers are not printed. He causes a minor furor in Canada and is accused of issuing a veiled threat when he tells *La Presse* in Montreal, "Some of our neighborhood associations have promised non-violent sabotage actions against companies who privatize and mine water on which we depend and which belongs to all of us.

The Diplomatic Council might not be able to dis-
suade them of such tactics."

1998 - After a narrow and contentious vote, bolstered by a high wave of student and youth
activism, and later by members of the island
IWW, the inhabitants of the archipelago approve
construction of a multipurpose stadium one-half
kilometer southwest of the harbor.

1999 - Danish and islander crews complete the
Stade de l'Ile (Island Stadium). The first event, a
concert by the band Rage against the Machine,
takes place before a capacity crowd on October 31,
1999.

<u>2000 – 93,452</u>

2000 - Competing for the first time in any international sports contest, a men's soccer team from
the archipelago represents Tiger Island at the
Olympic Games in Australia.

2002 - The Michigan Department of Environ-
mental Quality issues permits to Vevey Corp, the
largest water bottling company in the world, to
pump up to 400 gallons of water per minute
from aquifers that feed Lake Michigan. Tiger Island attorneys file suit in Michigan to halt the
company's operations.

2004 - The Men's Football Team of the Cooperative Commonwealth on the Tiger Islands wins the
Olympic Tournament in Athens, Greece and
takes home a gold medal. Prior to the gold medal
match, 13 of the 15 players on the Tiger Island roster wear black t-shirts; team captain Henri Sauvé

(b. 1983) states in a post-match press conference that the gesture is a protest against labor conditions which led to the deaths of 13 Olympic construction workers prior to the start of the games.

2005 - In April, Tiger Island F.C. begins match play as the 12th franchise in Major League Soccer, a professional league sanctioned by U.S. Soccer. Revenue from the club helps sustain the island's basic income, as of this writing.

2006 - In the wake of a Court of Appeals decision granting Vevey Corp the right to mine water from Lake Michigan and associated water tables, Tiger Island activists repeatedly sabotage equipment at Vevey Corp extraction points in Harbor Springs and Mecosta County, Michigan.

In May, masked arsonists torch a 50-foot-tall cartoon bunny-mascot at a Vevey Corp beverage distribution center in Anderson, Indiana. In response to the fire, Indiana governor Mitch Daniels (b. 1949) petitions the U.S. federal government to add Tiger Island to its list of terrorist states. The governor's request is denied by U.S. President George W. Bush (b. 1946) because no suspects had been named in the Indiana arson.

In July, a movement in which commonwealth cardholders play a key role succeeds with a historic community takeover of both the men's and women's sections of Paris Saint-Germain Football Club in Paris, France. The club restructures itself as a community and worker-owned industrial democracy; its profits and benefits are socialized among its workers and community stakeholders. Similar grassroots movements, aided by archipelago activists, develop around A.S. Saint-Etienne football club in France and the Seattle Mariners baseball team in the United States.

On November 12, Tiger Island F.C. defeats the Los Angeles Galaxy to win its first MLS championship.

2007 - In July, Commonwealth Cardholder Abeba Thomas-Dupont (b. 1968) signs with Crystal Palace Football Club (est. 1905) in London and becomes the first woman head manager in the history of the English Premier League.

On the evening of Friday, September 21, a weaponized TF-120 SkyViper drone devastates Tiger Island's indoor activity center and a large swath of the residential district, killing 1,766. No group or individual claims responsibility for the attack. Aid and supplies pour in from numerous parts of the globe. The GA commissions a task force to investigate and apprehend suspects. Western intelligence agencies and media rush to suspect Islamic Jihadists, citing the date of the attack, on Yom Kippur; the archipelago's proportionally large cultural and ethnic Ashkenazi Jewish population; and the virtual absence of practicing Muslims on the archipelago. (There is virtually no organized practice of any religion on the archipelago, apart from a nondenominational, spiritual ashram on Wind Island.) U. N. Peace-

keepers are temporarily deployed to the archipelago to ensure its security and sovereignty.

2009 - A staggering increase of cancers and birth
defects are reported on the island. A University of
Michigan study links the spike in cancers to the
depleted uranium bombs that fell during the 2007
drone attack.

2010 – 77,193

2010 - On October 27, tens of thousands of archipelago inhabitants help launch a Global Day of
Rage in conjunction with Amnesty International,
Human Rights Watch, and residents of Fallujah,
Iraq, who had also suffered a catastrophic spike in
cancers and birth defects following U.S. military
shelling of the city on multiple occasions in the
mid-2000s. An estimated 500 million people in
58 cities worldwide protest the manufacture of
depleted uranium and other munitions banned
by international legal agreements. On the same
day, tens of thousands of people around the world
engage in acts of civil disobedience against weapons manufacturers and Wall Street firms tied to
the 2008 global financial meltdown, leading to
hundreds of arrests.

2011 - On October 31 at 09:00 GMT -5, WikiLeaks and Project PM jointly release hundreds of
formerly encrypted emails sent in 2007 from the
vice-chairperson of Vevey Corp Waters North
America, Russell Edwards (b. 1950), to Charles
Nichols (b. 1969), CEO of the private military firm
Blackwater. The emails reveal a plot to attack

Tiger Island in response to repeated acts of "eco-terrorism" allegedly perpetrated by inhabitants of the archipelago. WikiLeaks also publishes Black-water invoices totaling $14 million for "deterrence services rendered" billed to a Vevey Corp shell company on the day of the attack. The revelations spark mass protests and boycotts against Vevey Corp in major cities around the world and lead to criminal arrests of six of its top executives. The Swiss corporation's future viability remains in jeopardy as of this writing. U.S. authorities arrest Nicholas in Virginia as he is attempting to board a flight to the United Arab Emirates, and they subsequently dissolve Blackwater's corporate charter, effectively blocking the organization from future licit operations.

The source of the Vevey Corp-Blackwater email hack has allegedly been traced back to computers at a building in Reykjavik, Iceland, leased by former Tiger Island soccer player and Olympic gold medalist Henri Sauvé. The U.S. government has charged Sauvé with serious crimes related to *The Computer Fraud and Abuse Act*, though his whereabouts remain unknown as of this writing.

the
BOOKWORM
box

Helping the community, one book at a time